bidisha

seahorses

Flamingo
An Imprint of HarperCollins*Publishers*

Flamingo
An Imprint of HarperCollins*Publishers*
77–85 Fulham Palace Road,
Hammersmith, London w6 8jb

Published by Flamingo 1997
1 3 5 7 9 8 6 4 2

The Publisher is grateful to the Marvell Press
for permission to use Philip Larkin's poem
'Deceptions', © the Marvell Press,
originally published in *The Less Deceived*.

ISBN 0 00 225440 9

Set in Sabon by
Rowland Phototypesetting Ltd,
Bury St Edmunds, Suffolk

Printed and bound in Great Britain by
Caledonian International Book Manufacturing Ltd, Glasgow

seahorses

Lonely in London? Want a lover? Want a life? First, get
the friends. You can do Coast, you can do the Groucho,
you can go up the Oxo, but you won't find what you're
looking for. Because you're looking in the wrong place. . .

They're all looking. Will, suave, predatory, cinematic,
has lots of sex, goes to loads of parties, but has no friends.
Well, just two. His Old Friend, Juliane, is a reclusive,
unproductive, misanthropic composer living out in the
Green Belt; his New Friend, Ian, skulks around the Top
end of the Piccadilly line with sights lowered. But when
Friends Old and New come together, a transformation
takes place. Meanwhile Will falls over and for a teenage
waif, Pale, a pretty, precocious schoolgirl with attitude
who shakes him out of his torpor and into feeling. And
the feeling proves infectious. New dawns rise for all. But
as dawn fades the dirty old town finds pretty much everyone tired of looking, always looking, when back at home
lies all the comfort and closeness you could ever desire. . .

Seahorses bobs through the dreams and nightmares of
this urban pageant with the utmost panache. It is a remark-
ably confident and mature debut, rich in bright imagery and
sharp observation, from a noteworthy new British writer.

BIDISHA is currently at Oxford University, having already
made her mark as a writer for the *NME*, *Dazed & Confused* and *The Big Issue* by the age of 16. This is her first
novel.

Seahorses

one

The dry indistinguishable stone fronts of the university buildings were vacant under a sun whose myopic eye surveyed London through its watery cataract. Will Corrin walked along Gower Street – one of these flat blank paths – one day in the first week of September.

He kept his eyes to the ground as his thinness snaked towards Dillons bookshop. That black suit, he knew, had been a purchase of genius, a – and this was one of his favourite phrases – a masterstroke of taste. In it, his back curved like the frame of a harp, his smooth head and soft slim hands jutted whitely, the flamingo legs in their shining ankle-boots snapped apart and together and propelled him across the pavement beneath strangers' glances of silent approval. In the damp and dark of the bookshop, where he imagined unseen fungus thickened behind pyramids of Travel Writing, mould

I

multiplied beside nests of Lit. Crit. and crept blue-fingered down shelves bulky with Hardy reprints, he glided, browsing. In one corner, alone, stood a little girl of about six reading a hardback. He watched her twist around on one heel in black pumps and scar-pink leggings, with hair the colour and gloss of piss, and could see through her T-shirt all the ridges of her neck and spine. He turned on his heel and walked back, towards daylight, past the red eye of the security camera and the blue doors.

His home in Bloomsbury, five minutes away: narrow, quiet, discreet. He rubbed himself in the hallway; the grey stonework received its occasional drenching, and drank it up greedily.

The flat had a clinical, celestial, mad look. It seemed to be enveloped and layered in white, as if wafered or pastried and rolled in rice paper, sifting and slipping like the torn-off scales of a fish. There were piles of notes and correspondence on the floor and desk and chairs, curled into a set of old box-files on the kitchen worktop and even slotted next to the breadbasket and stacked on top of the microwave. This was his work life: he was a film-maker of five years' experience. He wondered how the black knot of stamina, the glut of ideas and tight spring of creativity could mix and mesh and make so much papery disorder.

He had reason to be tired and to feel that, after thirty-eight years, something should ease. He'd read his Matthew Arnold and his Robert Browning and willingly bought into the old fantasy of a turbulent – and wrenchingly, dankly masculine – soul calmed by the touch of a pale hand or the gaze of limpid eyes, funnelling his romantic faith into a swampy imagined haven of Tennysonian passivity. Somewhere in his head was a mythological garden of content where long-haired girls in white cotton slips played tennis and drank tea all day, while swans bored sedately through impassive lakes full of Evian. Looking back now, it seemed that over the years he had slid, gnashing and grappling, into the clinging bear-nets of work and love affairs, somehow avoiding disaster. He had thought that life involved decisions, deliberation, required a super-consciousness as exact and objective as the working of a clock, and found only that it comprised slippery stone-pierced slopes, ditches rank with unseen red-gummed piranhas and, furthest on the horizon but advancing closer every choppy night, his own aged self, his own stark mortality, with its wrecked face and wasting muscles, its splayed feet and crinkling knees, the flapping buttocks and sapped virility, with its rusted tin brain rattling with the roasted beans of memory.

His prior history, then, hinted at a lack of direction. He had been a journalist, writing about fashion and film, had worked in advertising and graphic design, had reviewed art exhibitions and operas and even, in his more pristine days, modelled a little. In the last few years he'd made two reasonably successful films but the one he was currently working on, called *Electra's Dream*, was the testing-point of his talent. Looking at all the paper in his flat, which seemed to rise up and stick to him whenever he moved, and would glow with its own peculiar light first thing in the morning, he half-believingly set his heart on fame.

The first three weeks of September were taken up with meetings about *Electra's Dream*. He always worked from home, whose white paperiness he settled into, to forget about the rest of life. At night, though, the place would balloon and bloat and push him out, suffocated, into London. Masochistically interested, he came to see it, them – work and the flat – as an animal which consumed, masticated and digested and broke him down, expelled and then retook him at dawn. Struggling for his art in the clean-lined squares and streets of Bloomsbury, he liked to think of himself as professional fodder.

Tonight, Tuesday, was the opening of a new gallery in Covent Garden, as unique and pioneering and original as all the others. Everyone would be there, fangs just polished, claws newly sharpened. The creamy invite had arrived through the mysterious media network of coveted addresses only that morning; he'd come far, he thought, as he always thought, looking at the card's smug discreet message. From school and college in Kent, where he never made the effort, to London at nineteen, and on to work at a music paper. And then into a routine of concerts and parties, which had escalated.

He dressed and left the flat at nine-thirty. Bloomsbury's houses, coloured pastel pink, baby blue, mint green and soft grey, stood like lines of boiled sweets around graffiti-ed parks. He walked past Tottenham Court Road, through Soho, navigated Cambridge Circus, his clothes photograph-glossy. He saw himself in shop windows and the windscreens of passing cars, lean as an arrow, smooth as a gun's barrel.

The gallery was a frosty white set of rooms linked by high arches, glittering and sharply clean like the segments of a louse or the forever-searching eyes of a fly. So many people. Will saw in snapshots: a crushed red smash of lipstick in a kiss, several sets of broad sombre male shoulders, three dozen

4

bright rims of wine glasses and London voices full of paranoia. Will used to see a pattern in the decadence of the city: the same groups of acquaintances would disappear for a while and then resurface elsewhere, multiplying and spawning subgroups whose formation would bring on a wave of invitations to new places. Now all was incoherent, and the people who'd welcomed his company were replaced by a younger set who asked their friends, in Oxbridge voices, who the old man in the corner was.

Over an hour later, when the lights, paintings and smooth-planed faces had coalesced into a syrupy haze, he found himself with a young art student. The boy, whose name he had forgotten as soon as he heard it, was talking about a recent film in a shrill, oscillating, self-conscious voice; his right hip-bone pointed dramatically to the opposite corner of the room while his bared wrist orbited Will's glass; his shirt was a menstrual explosion of burgundies, his jacket an ejaculation of translucent creams, man-made and supremely flammable. Will looked over his shoulder and saw, in sudden sharp focus, that a pale thin woman in her mid-twenties was watching him from a few feet away.

He had slept with everyone. He would screw anything: ugly, old, ill. He had started at school, at fifteen, and coming to London had widened his horizons further. He took them home with him, or led them into the toilets at the venue, or into the streets if the area was empty and warm enough, or he went back to their flats. He fucked them the same way each time, learning and remembering nothing.

The routine of twenty years clicked into place and Will, comfortable in the role, glad at the opportunity, sped to the target. An hour after they met he asked her if she had any plans for the rest of the evening.

Of course they left together.

He felt, as they walked back to Bloomsbury and she put her hand into the crook of his arm – that was one of the best things about this jacket, no pawing woman could ruin its cut – for one moment, pleased, strong, worthy, revelling in the onslaught of male protectivity. But he screwed her anyway, and when the dead seven o'clock light changed the flat into an asylum-white cube, he told her to leave.

Later in the afternoon, when the columns of dates and details and numbers he needed to look over scrambled and undulated on the page, and the invisible malevolence of the flat began to prowl and circle around him, pawing and snorting, he too had to go.

At the same time, on the same Wednesday afternoon, a girl called Pale Jesson went shopping, a red plastic folder of completed essays in small square writing left in her locker. Being in the fifth year at school, GCSEs eight hazy months of B-grades away, meant that she could trawl the shops on her free afternoons. She walked out of the dark-porched Bastille and her sexless body with its dark hair and blank eyes, its calmly unruffled chest and flat haunches, made her look like a tiny hinged wooden doll clopping its way out of a shoe-box house.

She still had the money her father had given her when she turned fifteen three weeks ago; her mother had died when she was four, was ghostless and unvisiting, leaving no impression, no memory of a sweet touch on a forehead, an urged spoonful of cough mixture or gentle scolding, no memory of soft hands raking a scalp for nits. She thought of the shops in nearby Oxford Street and Covent Garden and the trashy-looking cinemas in Leicester Square as a second home. She walked the streets, feeling London's tenure, thinking that her disappearance would make no difference.

Covent Garden swallowed Will up in a flare of cobbles and market-stalls, and he watched the women going from boutique to café to bar, the sun lighting their hair copper, gold, jet and sometimes silver. He looked at their skin, the slopes of jaws and ears in downy white or gleaming brown, eyelids sometimes marked with kohl and shadow, and powder avalanching into the creases like sand in the narrowest dip of an hourglass.

He went to a bookshop on Long Acre, not a large store like the one of three weeks ago but a place which sold forgotten collections of literary criticism and poetry anthologies, recipebooks and abridged versions of *Jane Eyre*. Quickly becoming bored, walking past the shelves and finding that nothing appealed, he turned to leave, contemplating finding a café somewhere. He stopped at the Classics section for a moment and stooped, reaching for Dostoevsky on a low shelf, and accidentally pushed a girl who was kneeling on the floor by his feet, claiming the same book.

A bony shoulder was under his hand for one second, the velvet-covered hardness like the skull of a foal. Yeats bolted through his mind – 'A sudden blow, the great wings beating still / Above the staggering girl' – and was immediately blotted out by the crescendo; his heart had nothing to do with it, specifically, that sodden lump of palpitating horse-meat, it was the entire network of veins and arteries that loudened,

7

the synchronized stamp of a Nuremberg grinding in the pulse. She stood also and they both apologized, as strangers do, with averted eyes. She looked at him.

And there was a widening silence into which flooded soft heat, then a narrowed concentration, while the banks of colour on either side dissolved into a corrugated mirage, then vapour, and became soft walls of black; pure, sweet, unmarred with the hotly pumping fist of lust. Poetry in motion, said a stabbing, sardonic voice in his head. Tucked into the collective unconscious was the anticipation of a moment, a second devoid of conscience and simultaneously full of sensation, which, for Will, had now arrived.

And gone. The day's colours and noises – of the shop till, the cars outside, the shush of people moving past each other on the pavement – reasserted themselves, hard-angled and stolidly existent, with the hollow clang of quotidian routine, the uncomprehending moo of reality, for one second one-dimensional and then unfolding into three again, the gluey trance of the last moments breaking up and apart like a thousand released balloons separating in the air.

Pale stood in the bookshop watching the man go, with those thin boots rapping the pavement and the glittering studs in his cuffs each like a surfing body glimpsed in white sea-foam, and the dark-clothed form breaking cleanly through the cotton-wool vagueness of the crowd.

She thought she was nothing to look at. Flint-hard and pebble-cold, with coal-coloured eyes and skin clear and smooth but not glossy, like slate, she deviated too far from the ideal. Her face, tight as clay, had no expression. She saw the females around her and wondered what it would take to break out of the doll-shell into their lives, hammer red-nailed and bulge-eyed to stand oozing and panting in their reality; there was something between them and her, finer than a muslin curtain but more ferocious than a thousand-thickness of iron links, that she felt marked her out. And this bookshop beauty, the drama of only a moment, had cracked open something else she hadn't known about, because for her – if not for him – everything was in fact desire, everything was bodily sensation, she existed just to feel. And she felt she was too innocent.

She returned home to Ruislip, that leafily bland suburb in north-west London which was permanently sleepy with red wine and bad marriages and Sunday lunches and Valium, a few hours later; her father, who worked as a solicitor, was already there, immobile in his chair with the open carcass of a broadsheet on his lap. She put her school bag down in the hallway, throwing her coat on to the chair at the bottom of the stairs. She walked into the living-room and saw him, his luminous beauty, the creamy agelessness of a mannequin: silky-skinned, aggressively slim, imperial and serene, and only forty-one.

Nodding a greeting to him she went into the kitchen and, while making herself a sandwich, reasoned that not all men could be like her father. There must be something better, something more alive, to incite a kind of . . . passion. She liked passion, as she liked smut and scum, with their hissing and hot-breathed sounds, that whispered-in-the-dark for-biddenness, their tang of sleaze. She liked to hear about bang-ing and fucking and screwing, especially screwing, with its energetic and nocturnal undertone. She turned the words over in her mind furtively and sliced the wan white chicken on the board while her father, in the front room of the dolls' house, thought about how pretty she'd become.

two

The Lodge in Hertfordshire was a squat gravelly brown house. Its mossy haunches slid among deflated pillows of autumn mud and leaf; one coloured-glass window stared redly from the top floor, and London's clamour was lost in the countryside's spongy pink sky. Around it whined and clawed a permanent wind, dragging and pinching like thousands of tetanus jabs.

Inside, the Lodge was full of light, liquid-soft, as if a full womb had been pulled out and smashed apart: there were creamy floorboards, membrane-thin curtains, couches in velvet as pliable as jelly. At the end of the long hallway, past the closed door of the front room, was a severe white kitchen; to the right was a large white sitting-room with an archway leading through to the music room where, on a shaggy rug, were a closed violin case and a steel music-stand. A stone veranda at the back of the house looked out on to an Arcadian garden.

Juliane Morgan, thirty-nine, a composer, sat reading the paper at the white square table in the middle of the kitchen. He was dressed in narrow black trousers and a loose black shirt, his eyes' silver-grey tinge meeting a vein-blue border at the edge of the iris. His colourless face was pointed and crisp-featured, like a death-mask; his hair, black and copper like a pitbull, fell skewer-sleek to the nape of his neck.

Juliane hated the body, hated physicality. He preferred that his innards, rather than pulpy flesh, were made of glass pipes and pistons, an irrigation system of funnels, tubes and pipettes – as if Snow White had eaten her glass coffin.

He had no reason to be despondent; he was rich and successful. Since the time he graduated – Music, a First – he had composed countless scores for films, had recorded and performed his own work. His compositions, first released when he was twenty-two, were greeted ardently by critics. Every two years after that he produced more work, spending his twenties and early thirties working solidly, enjoying social London.

He stopped performing at the age of thirty-five. He was tired, he decided; he bought the house and settled alone. London was wearing itself down. One day, the people in the city would crumble to dust, buildings would sink into the ground, cars would shatter at the kerb. The pavements would melt, the sky would crease up and the capital would, in a pure white flame, burn itself out.

He turned the pages of the newspaper idly, having nearly come to the back cover, and hummed something summery.

*

Turnpike Lane was a dark forgotten part of north London, occupying the capital's periphery like a maggot on the carcass of a lion. It was a mesh of boarded-up houses, spraypaint-spattered railings, cracked paving-stones, abandoned cars, kebab shops, bagel shops, Indian grocers, harmless children's gangs, dangerous parks and barren gardens: a place where the alienated congregate.

It was the second week of September. Ian Litner sat in the front room of his home, his dough-face hidden behind a guillotine-blade of grey curtain. All around him was a humming: the walls of the terraced house, the old cars outside, the clots and gaggles of kids walking the streets, horns and sirens. Turnpike Lane, the forgotten end of the Piccadilly Line, was where the glamour and spark of the centre dulled and became unstoppable dirt and noise.

In the front room of Ian's house were no books, pictures or magazines, save the day's rolled-up paper on the floor. He was rocking slowly, his pasty neck and lank twists of mousey hair moving back and forth, at the wooden desk. He was working his way through the rewrite of a handbook giving instructions on the care and upkeep of a portable telephone.

He was a copywriter by profession, though he also worked in a second-hand bookshop near the house. He would usually go in three days a week to sort through new donations, kneeling on the ground flanked by the gauntlet of tall shelves with the guts of a brown cardboard box spread in front of him. It was always the same: Victorian novels, vast collections of Romantic poetry, some rogue copies of Byron or Shelley, and quite occasionally Blake. Once in a while kids from the local

13

comprehensive would drop in with cheap annotated editions of *A Midsummer Night's Dream* or *King Lear*.

The afternoon lumbered on; he worked and rocked, wrote and rocked, his slitty eyes fixed on the table, trying to ignore the humming of the outside world.

He had a powerful body. Twenty-seven years old, strong: a buffalo's haunches, forearms as silky as a panther's fur, chest wide like a stallion's flank, a python-long spine. But it was all hidden in puppy fat, like his legs, which resembled two rolls of pastry, and his face, which was bandaged in layers of extra skin. His wrists, whose tendons were as flexible and strong as a cat's, were cushioned in fleecy white mush; his eyes, which were fin-blue and sometimes algae-green, were surrounded and squeezed by the jellyfish-flesh on his face. He was boring and polite; people often wondered if he thought at all – whether he was conscious of himself.

His history was stark and full of pain, just like everyone's. He had been brought up in north London by his mother, with a half-sister called Sophie who was two years his junior. From the age of four he was identified as being a problem child, although his malady was never properly diagnosed. It had been referred to as laziness, fatigue, hypersensitivity, depression, backwardness and extreme introversion by his teachers. He left school and went to a poly where he worked through the Business Studies course and got his diploma without attending most of the lectures. His mother died of cancer when he was twenty-one and he felt his life beginning; he moved into this house and began a string of mid-level jobs.

Twilight in Turnpike Lane was not romantic. It seemed as though a drowsy shadow would stretch across the horizon –

slowly, streetlamps the colour of toffee-wrappers would become brighter, the noise of the children outside would deepen into the voices of older boys, McDonald's and the kebab places would fill – and then, suddenly, the day's light would be snapped off.

Ian sat back from his desk. The house, a 'large cool store', kept him dry and apart; he had everything he needed. He got up, went into the kitchen at the other end of the landing, and ate a slice of dry bread in the dark. On the worktop of the narrow kitchen was a hard white loaf, a shiny green box of tea-bags, a blue-striped carton of milk, a yellow economy tub of margarine and one knife. He walked from corner to corner, munching.

Back in the front room, something in the back of the paper caught his attention and his eyes narrowed for an instant in their sockets, like two marbles disappearing into the creases of a sofa.

It was getting dark earlier: London had about it a furtive look when, at five-thirty, boutiques' garish displays caught the eyes of shoppers fooled by the low navy sky. Across the city, people would walk out in the early evening telling their friends they could smell romance in the air, that this was the perfect time to fall in love, when a blue mist settled on the skin from late afternoon, deepening from cobalt gauze to lilac-silver brocade, then an endless train of royal purple silk.

On a Friday evening in the fourth week of September, Ian closed up the bookshop in Turnpike Lane and made his way home. He stepped past two young kissing couples, bomber-jacketed arms intertwined, and a herd of beige-raincoated

OAPs at the bus-stop. He arrived home and fitted his bulk into the slope of the grey sofa in the sparse living-room, thinking lazily of the thirty copies of *Brave New World* a peach-jumpered young teacher had slammed on to the counter tiredly that morning. He napped for two hours and was woken by the telephone ringing. It was Will: the two friends had not spoken in over a month and Ian's mind, sleep-muddy, was slow to recognize the voice.

Ian Litner and Will Corrin had met at a pub here in north London six years ago, the latter a journalist on a minor arts magazine; the former, who had just left the poly, into his second week at a bakery on the High Street. Neither had much money at the time, although Will's fortunes changed rapidly and within a year he would get into film.

Ian had been befriended by the boys he worked with, and they would take him to one of the three pubs on the High Street – the Dead Hart, the Beacon or the Virgin's Arms – after work. On one such outing he had looked past their dappled red skin and oily hair and seen Will leaning against the bar, dressed in his slim black suit, smoking.

Will had, that evening in the Dead Hart, whose furnishings were the colour of dried blood, been preparing himself for a fringe drama production. When he caught Ian's eye he was glad that even here he looked attractive.

Will's voice said over the telephone:
– 'So. What're you doing?'
– 'Just came home from work. Well, a couple of hours ago. I was taking a nap.'
– 'Oops. Thought you sounded sleepy. Can I come up anyway? I need some quiet company.'

– 'It was the Virgin's Arms last time, wasn't it? We can go to the Beacon, then. Is everything all right with you?'

Will's voice loudened then subsided formlessly in a yawn. He said:

– 'Tired.'

– 'You sound it.'

– 'Why don't you ever come up to town?'

– 'Too crowded, too dirty, too much trouble. We've had this conversation before.'

Will yawned again; Ian strained to understand him as he said:

– 'Whatever. What time do you want me?'

The Beacon was on the High Street, a peeling brown mock-fortress with walls scarred by old posters advertising gigs in the centre. Next to it, outside a yellow plastic fast-food place, was a group of fourteen- or fifteen-year-olds smoking and shouting at nothing; a few yards on, a thin old man in a faded grey suit, only one button done up, stood looking down the street talking to himself.

The Beacon was the darkest of the three pubs, with smoked-glass windows and large sturdy furniture. It was crowded: three listless students loitered by the jukebox while a young man in a leather jacket and white trainers played pinball; a flock of staff from a nearby estate agency sat trading insults about their boss; a brace of couples argued or said nothing to each other by the bar; a swarm of adolescent boys sat looking about.

Will was slung over his chair in the far corner, thin ankles crossed between slim black trousers and narrow shoes. The burgundy shirt, an embarrassed chutney of red cabbage and plum, was open at the neck. Like a schoolboy, he had taken off his tie and rolled it up, stuffing it into the pocket of the jacket which hung off the back of his chair. Although he had noticed Ian he looked away, perfect left-profile coming forward to light another cigarette.

After having got them both something to drink, Ian lowered himself cautiously into the seat opposite the film-maker, who leaned forward and said:

– 'How was work?'

– 'Quiet. School term's only just begun. In a few weeks they'll come in looking.'

– 'Let me guess. *Great Expectations*, *Wuthering Heights* – or *Jane Eyre* – and *Return of the Native*.'

Ian smiled, his round face splitting like curdling milk, and said:

– 'Probably. How's things with you?'

Will grimaced, making a gesture of helplessness, and whined:

– 'Hassle. You name it, I can guarantee it's not getting off the ground.'

– 'But, eventually . . .'

– 'Yeah. But it's waiting I can't stand.'

A loud male noise reared up in the far corner; Will and Ian turned to look at two teenagers, one in an oversized rugby shirt and black jeans, the other in a denim jacket and blue jeans, beginning to fight. On an unseen signal, following the old masculine code, they stopped suddenly, shook hands, grinned, clapped each other on the arm and separated. Ian watched with fear of the boys' pack-mentality, their unreality,

18

the unreadability of the allegiances; Will remembered his own youth and smiled to himself.

In a quiet voice, Ian said:

– 'I saw an advert for a job in the paper a couple of weeks ago.'

– 'Didn't know you were looking for one.'

– 'It caught my eye. I've been doing the bookshop and the writing for long enough now. And there're no prospects in work like that.'

– 'Will you apply?'

Ian shrugged, losing courage, and said:

– 'Thinking about it. The ad didn't say much. The person who placed it seemed quite indiscriminate. But it's probably not right for me.'

The film-maker looked at his friend narrowly.

– 'I thought you were happy as you are.'

Will didn't want Ian to change; the two men sat opposite each other, a white soufflé in loose khaki trousers and an ebony chopstick in a burgundy shirt. Their relationship thrived on differences.

The film-maker got up to order more drinks, his head light. Coming back to the table, where Ian was sitting staring into the ashtray, he said:

– 'I feel terrible.'

– 'Ill?'

– 'Tired. Probably more than I realized.'

With a sneer, Ian asked:

– 'Burning out?'

– 'At least burn-out's got some kudos. I'm just unfit.'

Two tall young men in business suits came into the pub;

people turned to look at them. They were model-perfect, from their Oxfords to their side-partings, lush coat-linings to manicured nails, with impassive faces, and they walked to the bar without speaking. Will eyed them jealously, hazily, from his corner. He said:

– 'I met someone a few weeks ago. A few days after the gallery opening I told you about.'

Ian looked up at him tiredly, sensing a monologue, but Will only added:

– 'A bookshop in Covent Garden. The cheap one on Long Acre.'

Will looked away, frustrated, and wondered how that stare of nearly a month ago could seem so real to him. He had always approached film-making with some irony, not believing that entire stories could be told soundlessly in the space of a glance, though looking back now he considered how . . . textured . . . the scene had been. Or perhaps he'd dreamt it, summoned it up in the dizzy gaseous dream-state of an alcoholic sleep, post-vomit. He and Ian carried on drinking, talking of mundane things, their thoughts not once connecting. He said, mainly to himself:

– 'I was just looking at the Classics shelves when I bumped into her.'

He grimaced to himself.

– 'I meet women all the time.'

– 'But this was different?'

Will nodded. Keeping his eyes on the table, Ian said:

– 'But then it could have meant nothing. To her.'

The noise in the Beacon had increased: the three youths had been joined by a group of friends mid-evening, of which the younger members were having trouble getting served; the close couples of earlier had begun to argue, while strangers flirted; the local office-workers were rowdy, in a haze of nylon skirts and polyester shirts, of sweat-circles and billowing ankles, court shoes and pop-sox. The two well-groomed young men were talking energetically, knees rubbing beneath the table, one pointing at a page in the open diary on the table between them. The room seemed to shift around Will; Ian's face was blurred. The film-maker said, beginning the conversation which ended all their meetings:

– 'I have to go home. The tubes don't run late up here.'

He stood up, gathering his coat and case. Making his way slowly across the pub to the door he said:

– 'It was good to see you.'

Ian, following Will out, asked:

– 'Will you call me again?'

– 'In a few weeks.'

Will opened the door and stood back against it:

– 'But I'm going to be busy with the film.'

Ian edged past him into the street:

– 'But you can call when you get a chance.'

– 'What's the point – you never come to the centre anyway.'

Will looked off down the street to the distant Underground sign.

– 'OK, I'll call you when I get the chance . . .'

– 'In a few weeks.'

With a nod and a half-touch, Will began to walk away. He called back:

– 'See you.'

Ian stood outside the Beacon, the night's black-gloved grip

hard on his shoulders, and watched his elegant friend walk up the High Street. The edge of the moon glowed hesitantly blue from behind a gob of cloud, like a baby smothered in its own bedclothes.

three

One Saturday afternoon in the first week of October, several weeks after the incident at the bookshop, Pale found herself in the National Gallery. Grey-walled and dim-lit from the outside, hunkering by the white stone edifices of Trafalgar Square and Pall Mall, it was a place in which to observe and consider. Inside, its vast-arched structure was softened by burgundy leather couches and honey-coloured wooden floors; a group of docile French students sat in a semi-circle around a large canvas depicting a hunting scene; a couple hugged before a picture of a girl in a white dress being led to the guillotine; a large American lady in late middle age gazed at a Degas nude bather.

Pale walked through white room after white room dressed in black leggings and a loose black shirt, stopping occasionally by a canvas. She had been letting homework pile up – there was a list of assignments she had to complete on her desk at home – but her mind was foggy and her thoughts as compressed as the air inside a bell jar: she couldn't concentrate. She walked on, past double-door after double-door, under the eyes of the security guards at each corner, until she came to the small red room at the end of the hall, from which no archway led on. On its crimson walls were smaller gold frames of reclining semi-nudes staring into the middle distance, an incongruous Goya war-scene in the corner, some woolly Bonnard portraits. Pale saw, with a feeling of sudden complication, the man from the bookshop. Although she at first noticed only the slope of his shoulder, the tight back and a sweep of hair across an ear, it was as if the final layer of wrapping on a half-expected gift had been torn aside. As if a child expecting to be hit finally feels the contact of palm and cheek.

His long black eye was following the silhouette of an oil breast, an acrylic thigh, a charcoal neck; he was dressed in slim indigo jeans and an old denim shirt, a teenager's rucksack slung over one shoulder. A cool blue column in the room's hot red, sleek as a bullet, he moved from painting to painting slowly; under the fluorescent lights his hair showed chestnut-brown, russet, gold with auburn streaks.

She tapped him on the arm. An image would stay with her for years afterwards: her fingers pallid against the blue cotton elbow, his slightly startled turn, her lurching step back and nervous

– 'We bumped into each other in the bookshop the other week. Do you remember?'

He looked down, at her hairline and brow, and replied:

– 'Of course. You were the innocent party.'

Stuck there, like a full stop at the end of a brilliant sentence, Pale looked away. She asked:

– 'Do you like these paintings?'

– 'Some of them.'

– 'You're not an artist?'

– 'I make films. I just come here to think.'

– 'So do I.'

She extended her hand again and said:

– 'Pale Jesson.'

Smirking slightly, seeing that the movement was unfamiliar to her, he took her hand.

– 'Will Corrin.'

– 'I've heard of you. From magazines.'

He looked at her, then away, through the door of the red room.

– 'Do you want to go for a coffee?'

Walking back down the salt-white rooms of paintings together, blue and black side-by-side like a bruise, they found they had nothing to say to each other. Like two toys – a tin soldier and a wood figurine – being marched down the aisle, they both stared ahead and stayed a foot apart. They went to the gallery café, buying sour coffee and sitting opposite each other at a relatively clean table; talked mechanically about school and work, joked about art, mentioned some recent films, each trying to make it easier for the other. The blood lava-hot in her veins, the hairs on her arms like fields of upright splinters, Pale softly put her black-booted foot on top of Will's.

*

Two and a half weeks ago Ian had seen the composer's advert; he'd done nothing about it. He spent the first week of October, whose grey-brown light had settled over Turnpike Lane like the skin on stale milk, behind the counter at the bookshop. Its grilled windows, low ceilings, tall wooden shelves and threadbare brown carpet made it look and smell like an old zoo-cage; the air was thick with flakes like rust in old water which stirred when people entered; visitors were heralded by the tired sound of a bell attached to the top of the door. The shop was a holding-tank for forgotten words, too-often-recited soliloquies, handicapped verse, difficult prose, outdated polemic, mawkish sonnets: somewhere literature was sent to live out its final days. With it Ian too was wasting, the light in his eyes onion-skin thin like the oldest pages, his body heavy and stolid as leather binding, the words he did utter faint like a rain-damped paragraph.

Isolation was not the ideal; safety was. He was young, and though part-way to the realization of a hermetic existence the outside still held some promise. Ian wanted only security; he was wary of stasis, of stagnation. If all ended in pain anyway, the ultimate choice lay between being a moving target and being a stationary one. He struggled through *Wuthering Heights* slowly, tucked into the coffin-sized slot behind the counter at the bookshop, and let his mind wander.

Something was swelling inside him. The phlegmatic whine of certain words and significant phrases would occasionally spear him as he looked through new donations for the shop – 'what clear stream / Shall with its murmur lull me into rest?'; 'the crime of being born / Blackens all our lot'; 'All is not sweet, all is not sound' – and a wave of grief at how much he had wasted pushed slowly through him like a blunt scythe-edge.

On Tuesday morning in the second week of October he got home and immediately went to sit at the desk in the front room. Taking from his notepad a single sheet he wrote a letter to Juliane Morgan. He pressed hard on the paper, his handwriting tiny and impeccable, no extravagant t-bars, flagrantly oversized dashes or vigorous commas. Like pennies stuck into a Christmas cake, there was hardness within Ian's personality; he wrote the persuasive note in a single draft, folded it crisply into thirds and put it into an envelope. He posted it the next morning and stopped thinking about it.

Friday morning stretched its cold limbs in Ian's bedroom, poking hard-nailed fingers of jaundice-yellow sunlight along the single bed, following the straight-backed chair and desk down between the grey floorboards, along the bare tan walls and past the damp on the ceiling. Ian did not have to go into the bookshop that day, and six hours of extensive rewriting (of a mail-order catalogue) last night meant that he slept late.

The phone – the old type, sitting like the corpse of a giant beetle on the desk – started ringing. The voice which greeted his cautious Hello? was dry and calm. So, Juliane was male; Ian felt something in his gut slide, like plates of land moving apart in an earthquake. The composer said:
– 'I was surprised to get your application.'
– 'You advertised.'
The voice laughed quietly.
– Nobody else replied. And it was a long shot. But I was glad to hear from you.'

There was a pause, during which Ian began to wonder if a trick was being played on him; he remembered Pinter's 'somebody is trying to do me in'. Juliane's voice mused:

– 'Fate, or something. Sorry, is it too early to call?'

– 'No. I was awake.'

– 'Are you interested in coming up to the house for a talk? I don't waste people's time.'

Ian said nothing, listening to the composer's waiting silence, feeling the soundlessness widen, until Juliane added:

– 'We can discuss it now, and you can decide how interested you are.'

The talk continued disjointedly for some minutes. Ian's voice, brittle and light as a toast-crumb, jerkily relayed his professional history, talked about music, described his daily life.

The composer's voice began telling him:

– 'I've been composing for more than fifteen years. People perform my work, I make recordings of it myself – I have a studio in my house.'

– 'You're very . . . successful?'

– 'I'm what you'd call distinguished. I should have been average or promising until a few years ago and then released my middle-aged masterwork on an unsuspecting public. Unfortunately, good fortune has always sought me out.'

– 'You still have the inclination to produce new work continually?'

– 'It's hardly difficult. You'd be surprised how boring it is. Someone, somewhere, will think the rubbish you make is worth framing or feting or publishing or promoting. Come and see me.'

– 'You live alone?'

There was another pause, and in that disturbing smug ironic tone the composer said:

– 'Splendid isolation. I've set myself beyond the pale. And all of that. How old are you?'

– 'Twenty-seven.'

– 'I'm thirty-nine. I used to be terrified of the outside. I'd go out and talk to everyone in the room – this is in the days when I took advantage of my reputation as classical music's great new talent, and made the brilliant move of adding that ambiguous "e" to my name, by the way, since I know you're wondering – and still feel that ... entrapment ... whenever anyone ventured too much into my space. A cliché, but then all clichés are true. In the end I made a decision.'

– 'Between?'

That baffling tone again.

– 'Rule of the mind versus the rule of the body. The battle of flesh and spirit. The eternal conflict. Have you never read a Hardy novel?'

– 'You chose work?'

– 'It's the simplest option. It doesn't make you go mad. Come to the house tomorrow. I'll tell you how to get here.'

Ian replaced the receiver when the call finished, Juliane's voice – dry as the sweep of fingertips on stone, as evenly controlled as the drop of water from a tap, an undertone like a cello-moan – echoing in his ears. The ulcer of melancholy in his stomach had an edge; Ian's comforting pattern of bookshop and writing was now vigorously cross-stitched with the prospect of new work. He spent the rest of Friday at home, completing outstanding work and writing letters of resignation to the agency which gave him copywriting work and to the owner of the bookshop; he didn't care what happened to the books, or who would take over the work he left behind. It was no longer his concern.

On Saturday he got dressed in his usual loose white jumper and khaki trousers, half-covered by a mustard cord jacket and black wool scarf. Closing his mind to the loose groups of family shoppers milling around in the sharp mid-morning air, he marched into the tube station at Turnpike Lane. He would have to travel to the northmost part of the network and then take a bus into Hertfordshire.

On the train his head felt light, as though the mass of his brain and the weight of his thoughts had been halved over-night; his throat seemed to have a sour metallic lining. He got off the train at Edgware and walked to the bus-stop. He could sense the city was shading away into woodland: the air had a base-note of damp soil, its eddies quick-changing and sweet-crisp; there were two pretty cafés and a post office beside a short parade of bay-windowed shops. Ian got on the bus; they passed a boot-maker, a newspaper stand and a tiny newsagents. Further on was a Catholic school, then an old church with its graves slanted like rows of fallen dominoes.

Ian got off the bus and began walking in the direction of Juliane's house. This part of the town was rich: he walked down the tree-lined street and passed yawning driveways lead-ing into secure private roads, seeing whitewashed, smooth houses with iron balconies, grainy brown houses with oak porches, massive irregular mock-Tudor houses. A dark green Jaguar slid into one garage; a burgundy Porsche eased out of a parking space; a bright, perfect family loaded tennis gear into their lilac space-mobile.

Slowly, the apparent affluence fell away. He followed a single curving route past walls of green that smelled thickly of decaying waste, and a wildness he pulled away from. He hoisted his pale leather bag under one arm as he came to the edge of the composer's property; the house was in front of him. On the left was the road by which he'd just approached and on the right he noticed woodland which raced to the horizon in glossy slats of eel-grey, shadow-black, kiwi-green and gold.

The front door was a massive slab of dark red wood – which reminded him for a moment of the blood-coloured furniture at the Dead Hart, where he had met Will – cool in the shadow of the porch. In the middle of the door was an iron knocker with the head of a cobra chipped into it, its hooded eyes both silly and unnerving. Ian's three knocks ran through the house and reverberated slowly back to him. Among the echoes he could hear light footsteps as someone approached.

Juliane opened the door and the two men, stunned, stared at each other. The dust of the porch – separated into colour-bands of syrup, honey, gold, lemon and pine – swam between them. Jasmine, honeysuckle and white roses, crawling confus-edly up a trellis by the door, released a burst of dense scent. Juliane looked delicate next to Ian's bulk, like a knitting needle left beside an oval of white wool. To Ian, the composer looked lizard-quick in his scale-green cotton shirt and slim black trousers, slanted silver eyes narrowing in a smile. He muttered faintly:

31

– 'Juliane Morgan?'

The small reptilian man smiled even wider.

– 'Were you expecting someone different? Do you still want the job now you've seen me?'

Ian smiled nervously and said:

– 'I need it, now. I've given up the other work I was doing.'

They didn't shake hands. Ian followed Juliane into the house; the hallway, slippery and white-brown like a maggot, was lined with mirrors and prints into whose frames photographs, notes, letters and reminders were stuck. On the floor were hundreds of thin volumes of sheet music: modern jazz for the saxophone, quartets for strings, woodwind and brass compositions, percussion studies. On the right, a wide wooden staircase swept to a white-railinged landing.

Ian followed the smooth line of Juliane's hair back down the hallway into the sitting room. The shelves set into the corners were stacked tightly with novels and books about politics, art, philosophy, history, all with cracked spines: Kissinger, A. J. P. Taylor, Calvocoressi; Hegel, Lacan, Freud, Jung; Paglia, Sontag, Greer; Proust, Milton, Dante, Spenser; Conrad, Kafka, Tolstoy; Morrison, Fowles, Ishiguro, Byatt, the expected Shakespeare, Dickens, Austen and Eliot; biographies of Dali, Gauguin, Kahlo, Monet, Rodin, Hockney. Ian entered the adjoining room by a smooth archway; laid there on the white rug was a violin case like an open wound, its velvet insides pale pink and slightly worn. The violin, an old Russian model, glowed red-brown like a coiled foetus in its rosy nest. The bow had been carelessly thrown down, and pointed across the floor towards his feet.

Juliane came forward to stand next to him and said:

– 'You were expecting a grand piano, weren't you?'

Ian said nothing.

The composer shrugged.

– 'I play everything. But the violin's what I play for my own . . . pleasure. I compose solo pieces, sometimes quartet or quintet arrangements, on the violin. The other stuff I'm commissioned to do is much less delicate: big film companies, big theatre groups, clans of TV people, orchestras who fancy a challenge.'

– 'But you prefer the violin?'

– 'For the simplicity. The fusion of player and played.'

Ian looked down at Juliane's sleek hair and asked:

– 'Is it emotional? For you?'

– 'No. But it's natural. More completeness than catharsis.'

The composer placed a smooth hand over his chest, indicating his heart, and said:

– 'No emotion left.'

– 'What made it go?'

A quick silvery smile.

– 'Nothing. It wasn't there in the first place.'

Ian walked around the room, circling the violin case, looking at the bookshelves and monochrome pictures on the walls.

– 'But you still play.'

An ambivalent, bored shrug.

– 'Oh, yes. To occupy myself.'

There was a pause, and the two men walked into the hallway. Ian looked at all the letters lying about, and said:

– 'You want me to clear all this up?'

– 'There're some important things there. Offers to use previously-recorded work, small commissioned pieces, some legal

33

wrangles over copyright, publishing rights and all the rest. Just come next week. On Monday.'

Ian traced a circle in a layer of dust on one of the glass tables in the hall.

– 'You just need a cleaner.'

– 'I can't talk to a cleaner. And you're here now. Starting Monday.'

A flippant smile and shrug.

– 'And I'm lonely.'

Monday morning in the third week of October was stormy; it seemed as though something slippery-black in the sky was clawing for escape. Bloomsbury was sodden, the toothpaste-coloured houses like a row of soggy party hats, the town-houses the colour of damp cardboard. Will, sitting at his desk in the paper-packed flat, stared at the phone. Dressed in fawn tracksuit-bottoms and a white long-sleeved top, he looked like a half-skinned chicken in a freezer. The phone had been silent for seven days; he tried to push *Electra's Dream* out of his mind.

He was at a critical stage in his career: people in the media had been watching him for nearly twenty years as he tried his hand at all possible jobs. They doubted his constancy; it was time he showed some direction. The industry he worked in had made it easy for him to not think; he had only to be graceful and funny, to pick up on cultural trends, coin a snappy phrase, fuck enough.

He reached over with a jolt, picked up the receiver, dialled half of Pale's number, then hung up. Fear and embarrassment shut down on him, preventing him from ringing again. He thought about it, about Milton's 'dark, dark, dark, amid the blaze of noon' when they first saw each other, and Larkin's 'spring-woken tree' in her glance. She was small, fine, clean and intact, like a full moon's perfect circle.

A second spark, an echo of the earlier, and boredom, propelled him into calling Ian. He asked:

– 'Doing anything this afternoon? Aren't you just staying at home?'

There was a pause, in which Will heard Ian shift in his seat, move some rustling objects by the phone, begin saying something then stop, and finally reply:

– 'I might have to be somewhere. Work. What're you doing?'

Will looked round the flat, idly flipped the cover of a notebook open, turned and lowered the volume on the stereo, and said:

– 'Sitting about at home waiting for someone to call.'

He added:

– 'What kind of work?'

– 'The job I told you about.'

Will stretched, half-yawned, listened for the new timbre in his friend's voice. He said:

– 'Well, give me the details.'

– 'It might not work out. It's a composer called Juliane Morgan.'

Something flared momentarily in Will's head, like the sudden new blaze of a chameleon's skin. He asked:

– 'Where does he live?'

– 'Hertfordshire. I went to see him there at the end of last week.'

Will looked round the Bloomsbury flat, which blurred and

pulsed for a second, like an eel moving through a muddy
sea-floor; he said:
– 'I used to know him.'

Ian's voice sounded distant – he seemed to be holding the
receiver far from himself.
– 'You used to know everyone. I have to go soon.'
– 'Will you do something for me? Give me his address?'

By way of explanation, of excuse, he added:
– 'We did use to be friends.'

Will listened to the burr of the disconnected line some time
after the call had ended: it mutated into the sound of teeth
grinding, the crunch of tyres on gravel, the fuzz of a badly-
tuned radio.

He and Juliane Morgan had been close nearly ten years ago,
having met at a launch party for a project which the latter
had been working on, the former reviewing. In the winters of
their three-year friendship they had stayed indoors, usually at
Juliane's flat, listening to music, drinking and talking. In the
evenings, they would venture out for dinner, and then a func-
tion. In the summers they had gone for half-hearted runs, had
breakfast together in town, spent the days that they weren't
working going to the cinema, seeing exhibitions or plays, letting London into their blood. There had been some bad
moments, which Will's mind twisted smaller and tighter out
of remembrance. Juliane had moved to a different place, and
slowly they had lost touch.

There was a wrenching noise above, and the cement-grey
wall of cloud burst, lightning-streaked, like a vicious second
dawn.

*

A sheep forgotten by the flock, Ian's fleecy form meandered up the hill towards the Lodge on Monday. He felt his skin crawl as he heard the leaves moving over the ground by the house, the wind through autumn trees like the wet whisper of a snake shedding its skin.

Juliane opened the door while he was still ambling up the path. The composer was dressed in a loose shirt with a touch of moss, a cardigan with slate-grey stitching, dolphin-blue slim jeans; he had even muttered a self-congratulatory 'a veritable little Pan' to his reflection that morning. His feet, intricate and soft white as spiders' webs, were bare. When Ian arrived, slightly out of breath, sweating a bit, he smiled and said:

– 'Twenty minutes late on your first day.'

'Sorry . . .'

Ian waited for Juliane to step aside and give him space to enter.

– 'Somebody called me –'

Juliane waved a hand nonchalantly.

– 'Don't worry about it.'

– 'Actually, he said he knew you. Will Corrin.'

The name glimmered senselessly in the composer's mind. Eventually he shrugged and said:

– 'A journalist I met once.'

– 'Film-maker, now. For five years.'

Juliane raised an eyebrow, made a gesture of mild surprise and asked:

– 'Did he say anything about me?'

– 'No –'

Ian remembered and then blushed.

– 'But I gave him your address.'

The composer's hand-wave again, like the slow dip of a white flag.

– 'It makes no difference. But I generally prefer not to commune with the past.'

He grinned, turning into the hallway of the house and indicating that Ian should follow. Ian closed the door behind them and put his bag down in the hall, at the base of the stairs. Taking off his jacket and putting it on the banister, he remarked:

– 'Will's interested in you.'

Juliane led Ian down the hall into the white kitchen and said over his shoulder:

– 'The feeling isn't mutual. But is he still in London?'

In response to Ian's nod he said:

– 'Land of hope and glory! It's amazing he still believes the myth.'

He went to stand by the sink in front of the window. Glancing back at Ian he asked:

– 'Living alone?'

Ian took a seat at the small white table in the middle of the kitchen. He nodded.

– 'He doesn't like it.'

Juliane fetched two black mugs from the rack by the sink.

– 'Girlfriends?'

– 'Sort of.'

– 'What does he call them?'

– 'Screws.'

– 'Always was a charmer. Whereabouts in London?'

– 'Bloomsbury.'

The snap of the kettle.

– 'He's done well. He was a hack when I knew him. He drank and fucked, just like everybody else. He worked hard, when he had a passion for something. He had potential.'

He took two mugs of tea over to the table where Ian was sitting.

– 'I don't like it when the past comes back. Buried memories revert to life. Suddenly you remember yourself ten years younger, naive. And of course it's too late.'

The sardonic voice, a mocking grimace.

– 'Life gets you down.'

They drank their tea, the sweat on Ian's arms and back evaporating slowly, his short thin hair flopping and puffing about his head. He looked at the composer who sat like a cricket, with his legs folded up on the seat. He must be no more than five foot eight, Ian thought, and yet his body held the potential strength of a sprung man-trap, becoming more sinewy with age. The composer's eyes swept around the kitchen, allowing his new employee the chance to look at him. There were mugs on the rack by the sink, a small pile of drying plates next to it, tall cylindrical jars containing cereals, lentils, pasta along high glass shelves. Juliane said:

– 'I live in my own world. The nuclear family, without the family.'

He smiled frivolously, incorporating a shrug and a baffled brow-crinkle.

– 'A monk without the religion.'

Ian asked:

– 'Was there once a family?'

– 'There was a wife a long time ago. We met by chance. She was clever and studious and introverted.'

39

– 'How did –'
– 'She killed herself, of course.'

Juliane paused, without mirth, and said:
– 'That'll give you something to mull over.'

He was quiet again, until:
– 'Don't tell Will. He doesn't know.'

Ian kept his eyes on the table, avoiding Juliane's look like a maggot curving away from a fishing-hook. After a while he said:
– 'This is a big house for you to live in alone.'
– 'It needs to be. I spend my life here.'
– 'I prefer things small and secure.'
– 'London's the parasite. "Something is rotten in the state of . . ." Well, eventually you have to move.'

Standing up suddenly he said:
– 'I'll show you where you'll be working.'

They went back up the hallway and passed, on their left, the rooms Ian had seen on his first visit. Through the archway at the back of the living-room he saw for an instant the music-stand and the violin case. He followed the composer through the first door in the hallway – something he hadn't noticed before – into a small room. Its almost perfectly square proportions and the high picture-rail made it seem like a dark lidded box: in front of the dirt-edged window was an oak desk the size of a butcher's bench; on one wall a mirror with a gilt frame oppressed the curlicues of the dusty mantelpiece, while the adjacent wall was smothered by a ceiling-high book-case. Ian noticed rows and rows of poetry in familiar leather binding: Coleridge, Wordsworth, Marlowe, Donne, Clare,

Pope, Herbert, Herrick, Dryden, Keats. He walked into the centre of the room. Juliane was saying:

– 'Take in all the business letters. Don't say yes to anything that means I have to be away for long. I can go to the city for meetings, but if I work, I work here.'

Ian sat down in the large oak chair by the desk.

– 'What else?'

There was a pause. Juliane finally answered:

– 'Anything that needs to be done.'

– 'Are you sure I'll have enough to do all day?'

– 'I'm sure we can find something to occupy your time.'

Juliane turned away and Ian realized that he really had no other job. He looked out of the window at the gravel path and girdle of trees fading into a distant green-grey smudge. The composer said:

– 'It might turn out to be interesting.'

Ian laughed and said lightly:

– 'How interesting is anything?'

Juliane turned back to him, acknowledging the rhetoric, and answered:

– 'I have a whole routine on that topic, complete with ironic jokes and humorous asides. But I'll spare you.'

Ian was getting out of his chair:

– 'I'll come tomorrow at . . . nine?'

– 'Best make that eleven.'

– 'You're not up earlier?'

A smooth shrug, reminding Ian of the surrounding landscape's sleepy roll.

– 'Yes, but I need the house to myself.'

Juliane walked over to the mirror and inspected his face. To himself, he declared:
– 'How the mighty are fallen!'
He gave Ian a sidelong look.
– 'You can do it, can't you?'
Ian walked out of the front room. Getting his bag and coat, he said:
– 'Yes, of course.'
Juliane opened the front door for his new assistant.
– 'Take care.'
– 'See you tomorrow. Thanks –'
The composer slammed the door on Ian's heels.
– '– Juliane.'
It was noon. The autumn sun, its curve slash-fine, pulsed over the patchwork of ochre and green. The wind-moved land-scape rippled like a cobra's hood as Ian walked away from the Lodge. As if each nerve had been balanced on point, he thought he could sense the gradual pull and constriction of London as he sat on the bus and train. Even though he himself was on the edge, the cracks and dirt-patches, the way every-thing looked as if it was covered in grey dust, the sense of toxicity under the liveliness led him to half-believe the composer.

The house in Turnpike Lane was dark; not the tarred black of Juliane's hair or the glossy pitch of a night in the countryside but rusty, 'muddy-mettled' and edgy. Lying on the doormat as he entered he saw, shining like the eyeball of a mad dog, a slim white envelope with familiar writing on it.

Sophie Litner. Twenty-five years old. Ian's half-sister. She was married now, to John. So she was anonymous Sophie

Brown. She lived in south London, in a big, ugly, dead district. He began to read.

I know we never speak. For some reason we've always stayed away from each other. We never did seem to get on – or perhaps we never tried – I don't remember. Why haven't you moved away? The same old shops, the same three pubs, the tube station. They never change.

I'm writing this at the kitchen table. It's past midnight. John's in bed. I can't blame him – he works hard. He's on the council now. Fulham Council – always in meetings. Always working late. He talks a lot about responsibility and duty.

I need your help. Things are bad. I've made a mistake. I must see you. Nothing in my life is as it should be. Things have slipped.

He checks everything I do. I can't go out of the house, except to shop ... he gives me money to spend on food, and a list of things he wants. He won't let me read books. You know I used to like writing? Maybe you don't. I kept a diary. Little stories, some poems – nothing very interesting – I don't write about the horrors of my life – he found it. Burnt it – nice and primal, nice and basic. He didn't even shout. Just one of those things.

I tried to draw, too. Always had a talent for it. Something else you don't know. Sometimes I even drew John. When he was asleep and I couldn't relax, I got out of bed and drew him. Funny how we immortalize what we hate.

He's jealous of me. It's got worse. He always suspected I was better than him. I am. More intelligent at least. The

43

cliché: I see more, because I know what pain is. Married at nineteen. What a fool. He's hit me, of course. Even though I expected it, I waited for it, it surprised me.

Can I come and see you? You know I wouldn't ask if it wasn't an emergency. It's mid-October now. I can't face Christmas with John unless I've decided something. I need to see you soon. I have to make a decision. He won't follow – he's always been wary of you.

What about your life? I hope you've found someone. Someone to be with. I can't imagine it. But don't we all fall for it? I hope you're not like me. I envy you, then, if you've never loved.

I'll try and call you when John's out. I hope you'll let me see you. I'm sure you understand –

Until we speak

Sophie.

The rusty dark of the house breathed and shifted around him. He remembered with distaste the tall girl with soft chocolaty hair, nervous eyes like two brown beads and a thin mouth. She had a brittle voice and a skittish manner, moving like a duckling caught in the furrows of lake-water. The cool hysteria in the letter, so unlike Ian's placid manner, assaulted this image, the pain in it being rip-keen and acid-bitter.

He had never understood love, hating its unseen complexity. He looked at the letter, comprehended that he was involved, now, in something hurt-soaked, opaque-surfaced.

four

Pale was in her bedroom on the Friday evening after the National Gallery meeting. The Ruislip street glowered thickly in the dark; she could look out and see all the damp wide slate roofs, the wooden porches, thick gravel driveways, corrugated black-doored garages, the mock-latticework over the windows, the safe network of intercoms and house-alarms.

The room was small, narrow, functional: a tan cord carpet, bare white walls and a pine bed; a square window above the pine desk looked on to the street; one tall set of shelves held a radio, a shoe-box full of tapes, a multicoloured row of bottles, hairbrushes and creams and a few books which she had been reading for school: Eliot's *Middlemarch*, Hardy's *Jude the Obscure*, Austen's *Emma* and a vast hardback of Shakespeare's Complete Works left open at the first page of *Measure for Measure*.

She lay on her bed in a black tracksuit, her hair thrown out to one side, a few locks of it falling across her neck and chest. She liked her Lady Godiva hair, Venusian, the way she'd come into the room after just having showered with it like a black cape, water-glossed and smelling clean-sweet, around her collarbone, over her breasts and between her shoulder-blades. It would take hours to dry, sifting and gathering, then deepening into jewel-shades and tapestry-colours: tar black, brown like mahogany, walnuts and rain-smooth mud, with lines of blood red, rust, ruby.

She looked at the ceiling, watching a tiny gold-burgundy spider scuttle haphazardly in a corner, wondering what would happen the coming weekend. Her thoughts started small: she would finally go and buy *The Information* or *The Moor's Last Sigh*; she would go and watch a film; she would take a walk and have coffee in town. But each grim isolated idea would fill, swell and rise, her head emptied; she found herself thinking of the blue slope of Will's back, of the warm roughness of denim, the tightness of his forearms, like soft white leather, his occasionally-caught smell, which was male and pungent but glossed over with Paco Rabanne aftershave, the lurching of the red room when she saw him, the fading and blackening of the bookshop when they had first met.

Will was an emblem of the outside: he aggravated her, his weight, the totality of his existence, the responsibility of it. She wondered what she was supposed to feel; in her classes they trudged through *Women in Love* wearily, plundering also *A Room with a View*, *Jane Eyre* and *Roxana* for essays on passion; she could no longer identify any of what she read, however diverse, with what she was feeling, which was nausea, fear, claustrophobia, the beginnings of a long tiredness.

He called at ten-thirty, the time men always call initially, before the midnight discussions and soft mid-dawn talks, before the freak single-rings and missed appointments, and the hanging-up. They talked for a dry half-hour: it was banal and strained; there was an attraction; they planned to meet again. She thought about sex, wondered how she could avoid it, resigned herself to it, quailed at the inevitability, and waited.

Will watched October wrinkle and finally subside from his bedroom window every morning, its bland shuttered largeness opening on to vivid colour, the white-walled room a migraine-throb of dawn light. He would lie in bed looking at the rumpled flesh-pink and chilblain-blue sky or, if it was raining, folds and folds of limp cloud padding and prodding into Bloomsbury's houses.

He and Pale had been seeing each other over the last two weeks; he had dreamed about her four times in a row now, lucidly, unimaginatively and intricately. He gave himself up to the new obsession and, in the end, thought more about himself than about her, feeling that the nocturnal sequence of phone calls, meetings, visions and sudden thoughts bubbling up mid-work signified a new psychological layer developing between him and others. He became, through his devotions, more complex, more interesting to himself.

Alone, he occasionally allowed his thoughts to bob and skim blindly beside the more grim-shadowed banks of the affair; he hated ambiguity, he hated not knowing something; obliqueness and obscurity puzzled him. It was easier to idealize and cement the gaps in his knowledge with metaphor or cliché, with the surface, such as the gossamer-fine grain of her skin, the hands and feet like willow leaves, the flimsy sallow straight-limbed body, her waves and waves of endless silence.

He had to fuck her; he was waiting, and they both knew that his delicacy, his politeness, the aura of innocent wide-eyed sweet-lipped newness, wouldn't endure.

Electra's Dream, his magnum opus, wedged and glowered in his conscience, black and steep-peaked before the frilled pink mist of his romance. He felt the threat of its enormity but didn't understand the form of its growth; he saw the minute obstacles, the finest cracks and cavities before his face but looked desperately for the middle path, progression, and saw no easy route. Filming would be starting soon – he couldn't remember when exactly this had been decided – and contracts had somehow been drawn up, schedules confirmed, finances backing equipment, sound, lighting . . .

Art is lonely, he thought to himself. Genius is lonely, his ego tentatively suggested. The dozens of people he employed waited for his word, exerting unseen pressure, whisper-quiet but gale-strong; he felt at once isolated, thinking tired thoughts, dull-minded, and urged on further by something unnameable and massive, mysterious, flaming and careering, tornado-intent. Creation is a peculiar process, he said resentfully to himself, he said comically to friends, he said drily, with a note of irony, to colleagues. The artisan and the art, he mused inconclusively, the specific becomes the general, the physical the spiritual.

So he had a life, with its massive clichéd metaphors – the terrible mountain of Art, the radiant new lands of Love, the invisible pressures of Responsibility – and was still lonely, a tragic–heroic apogee of John Clare's stark, 'I am: yet what I am none cares or knows'. In the end he could only conclude, masochistically: We are our own gaolers; we create a past we grow to hate, and we place in it things we know we cannot forget.

On the Friday evening in the last week of October, Will sat on a cushion in the middle of his white-stacked flat, writing his important Musings down on the pad balanced on his knees. In his stylish lolloping right-leaning script, he made the progression from present to historic, scratching out, 'I know I haven't been in touch', and, 'Do you remember me', and, 'Well, enough of my news'. Although it was only five o'clock, the street outside was a cool formica-smooth black; Bloomsbury's brown town-houses stared at each other rigidly while the candy-coloured homes glimmered palely in the dark like fallen confetti. Will had lit candles around the flat, softening the crisp-lined bales of notepads, books, letters, the computer hardware, the sheafs of Post-its, old faxes, reminders, newspapers; all had been enveloped in creamy honeyish light, lost some definition, became a glowing papery meringue, a whipped cream éclair of timetables and printouts.

The candles burned down; seven, then eight o'clock passed; the light PVC-black of early evening acquired the dense matt rubbery pressure of night, airless; the rumpled pile of notepaper next to Will grew, toppled, fanned out. He wrote, 'I've heard you settled down', and, 'Well, things have been going quite well for me', and, 'Funny how things turn out', crossed it all out, threw the paper away, started again.

*

The next night, north London's sky came out clothed in a ragged harlequin's suit of sable brown, charcoal grey and slug-black. Groups of seventeen- and eighteen-year-old girls walked to the tube station wearing hipster trousers and silly slinky strappy sandals, slim-fitting satin shirts under their long coats or puffy jackets; the younger kids spilled out, as usual, on to the High Street, catching a film at the Cannon on the corner then having a burger and a smoke.

The Dead Hart pub used to be white, with tiny turrets and wavy stone fringing beside the wide bay-windows; in the summer, its narrow crazy-paved front patio had been decorated by baskets and tubs and trellises of flowers, violet-pink, red-gold, yellow-blue, and on each of the glossy broad picnic tables had been a green glass bowl of ivory-coloured roses. These days, its rain-grey walls were edged with blue-green mould, brownish damp, black grime; the patio was bare, a fortress of empty beer cans in the corner lapped by nightly tides of fast-food wrappers.

Inside, all was soft, formless, sagging and depleted; nothing matched anything else. Will sat on a peculiar furry brown love-seat looking around at the motley collection of stools, armchairs, benches and ledges, seeing chipboard mixed with threadbare velvet, foam, stained silk, oak, a few tacky incongruous folding chairs. Only the large barren fireplace and fading delicate floral wallpaper, depicting studies of lilies and orchids, indicated the original elegance.

Will was dressed casually, tiredly, in black jeans and a loose navy fisherman's sweater, his expensive rough wool winter jacket in a dark heap next to him. He'd had his hair cut that morning; it was blunt, marginally too short and sharp, it had lost its movement. His face was scored with new cracks, temporary but deep, like the cleavage of scorched ground during a drought, surrounding the plump lips and underlining the black eyes. He looked, appropriately, like a Hallowe'en figure, the macabre Epstein sculpture, 'The Rock Drill', a death's-head on a scarecrow body.

The pub was not truly empty but occupied by disintegrating, deteriorating people, flaking away. In the corner next to Will, on the other side of the fireplace, a middle-aged pair sat, both with patchy red skin and lank spaniel-brown hair; three old men sat on tall wooden chairs by the bar, one wearing a slate-grey jacket and beige trousers, another all in olive-green tweed, with shiny patches on the knees and elbows, the third one in a powder-blue V-necked jumper and creased black trousers; at the far end of the room, amidst the soft debris of several carrier bags, sat a deflated-looking woman of about forty-five, whose puffy face had held on to the last remnants of grave good looks though her neck was folded over the collar of her labrador-gold nylon jacket and her corned-beef calves quivered beneath the hem of a navy pleated skirt.

Ian walked in looking festive, large, comical, in new forest-green cords, shiny brown leather shoes and a loose startling squarish jumper. It was the first time Will had seen him in dark colours; he was accustomed to a fey and baggy palette of khaki, cream, sage green, aqua-blue, soft grey and fawn cotton, linen and lambswool. Ian's hair, the sweetly bristled soft fur, had now been cropped severely; his scalp looked white and hard, army-tough, crocodile-tooth vicious. Will noticed the small close-set eyes of the barmaid, with her greasy brown ponytail and bulging silky blouse, following his friend's wide back over to his corner.

Ian sat down in the oak chair opposite the love-seat, easing into the lean frame with its padded leather back-rest and smelling the expected rising scent of flesh, mustiness, spice and varnish. He noticed the dry brittleness of Will's skin, realizing with a little snap of obscure pleasure that more than a decade divided them. He smiled in acknowledgement of the pint that sat ready in front of him; Will watched the way he picked it up, the massive-knuckled white fist curled around the base, creamy against the drink's thick black, and almost girlishly tilted his head back, shutting his eyes as he drank, sweetly kissing the edge of the glass.

Will said:

– 'You look good. It's the first time I've seen you in such rich colours.'

– 'I needed a change. I haven't bought myself anything in a long time. I went to the shop and somehow I couldn't bear to get any more of those loose pale trousers or white jumpers. I saw this red, the way the different shades of it were mixed together, and bought it on impulse. And the hair was getting on my nerves. It reminded me of a kitten's, just soft and useless, so I had it cropped as closely as I could. I can't decide what I think of myself. I get a shock every time I look in the mirror.'

Ian ran a hand across his head, feeling the soft fuzz under the pads of his fingers, making what he thought was a funny confused face at his friend. What Will saw was different: a marginally leaner face, brutally shaven-headed, strong-jawed, wide, with copper-sulphate-coloured eyes, crystal-hard, crystal-bright. There was still fat, open-pored and cling-ing thickly, but the haircut and dark clothes led to a paring-down of the overall image. The film-maker made no comment, aware that he looked bad, his skin as grey and grainy as cigarette ash. Ian cleared his throat, edged his chair closer to the table, ran his eyes over his friend's half-reclining black wool body in the love-seat, placed his hands on the table, around the bottom of his glass, and said:

– 'My half-sister Sophie who married John when she was nineteen six years ago might be coming to stay with me because they're breaking up.'

He took a breath and added:

– 'And I don't want her to.'

It was impossible for Will to imagine Ian's inner life, to consider if there were tunnels and teeming flurries and electric-fast flashes of thought behind the impassive wide shield of that forehead, conflicting and haranguing or harmonizing and soaring Musings like his own pulsing at the temples. He remembered Ian having mentioned a half-sister once, years ago, perhaps their first ever meeting, but the information had sunk, silent-soft, as if into quicksand. Ian was saying:

– 'She has no right to get in touch with me.'

Will said nothing. He got up to get more drinks, edging past the three men at the bar, smiling genially at the barmaid – who didn't find him attractive, he noticed – and waited. He turned his head, seeing the back of his friend's frame curved over as he had left it, elbows on the table, gazing into the distance, a lonely giant. But the film-maker had nothing to say, was too full of the hot thick soup of his own experiences, except, dumbly, when he got back:

– 'I knew from the moment you walked in that it was going to be a strange night.'

He looked down, immediately saying:

– 'Sorry. I didn't mean to be flippant.'

Ian shrugged.

– 'She wrote me a long letter telling me she was in trouble, and that she needed a place to stay.'

– 'And you don't want her to?'

Ian made a gesture of disgust.

– 'I know I'm the last person she can turn to. Neither of us ever made friends easily, or I suppose her friends can't hide her from John, they live too close, but . . . I'm being childish, I know. Nobody has ever come into my house or lived with me since I moved in. I've got to help her, there's no way I can refuse, but I don't want to. I read her letter and a part of me was sorry for her, there was something so pathetic in that request for help, and at exactly the same time another part of me just didn't care.'

Will nodded sympathetically this time, a safe gesture, and said tritely:

– 'You said it yourself. You're the only one she can go to, and there is such a thing as family loyalty. If her husband's being cruel you should want to help her.'

There was a pause. The barmaid dropped a glass and muttered, 'Shit' in the ensuing silence. Will said:

– 'I'm surprised. It's almost as if you don't mind him mistreating her.'

Ian grimaced.

– 'Part of me feels I should defend her, the other part just . . . it sounds bad, I know it does . . . I haven't seen her in a long time.'

He looked up at Will.

– 'You don't get upset if you hear about killings and beatings on the news, do you? She's as close to me as that. A face I vaguely remember, handwriting I vaguely recognize.'

He sighed, finishing off his second pint, his throat working vigorously.

– 'Sorry I mentioned it. I wasn't looking for approval or disapproval or advice. It was just on my mind.'

– 'When does she arrive? Did she say?'

– 'She said in her letter that she'll call me.'

Ian reached across for Will's now-empty second glass, arranging the four around the ashtray in the middle of the table, separating them to form the points of a square, placing them in a straight line.

– 'So now all the time I'm at home I can't relax properly. I keep thinking the telephone will ring and it'll be her at the tube station here asking for me to walk up and meet her. Or I hope she'll call to say it's all been sorted out.'

He crashed the four pint glasses together.

– 'Sorry, anyway. I don't like bothering people with my problems.'

Will laughed nervously, trying to lighten the tone.

– 'People? I'm getting jealous. What other friends do you have?'

Ian laughed in kind, acknowledging the attempt, until they both raised their heads and looked at each other, remembered, and were silent again. Ian got up, stretched, went to get more drinks, smiling patiently as the barmaid preened and whinnied and winked bafflingly at him. He saw his near-bald pillowy head in the mirror behind the bar – it was better than he expected – and caught, minute behind him in the reflection, Will's face, watching him, tight-featured, hostile.

He returned with the drinks. Will said, casually:

– 'So, you're working at Juliane Morgan's now?'

– 'Every day.'

They looked at each other, guarded, hearing and not turning at the sound of the barmaid breaking another glass, and Ian added:

– 'He's clever and sharp and smug and I think I could learn a lot from him. I'm just organizing his things, a sort of secretary, but he's talkative and funny and . . . he challenges me.'

– 'I know.'

Ian heard the soft bottom-note of Will's voice, viola-sombre, and recognized something time-hidden, regretful. The film-maker asked:

– 'Does he talk about me?'

Ian nodded, then shrugged, unable to lie.

– 'He asked how you were. He wishes you luck. I told him you were making films and he said he was relieved that you were finally doing what you want to. He said you'd been drifting for two decades.'

This reality, spoken, was hurtful. The past comes back to tell the truth, as a marker, a spirit-level of progress, to make us face what we would rather not, Will noted internally. He asked:

– 'What does he look like now?'

– 'Probably no different to how he looked when you knew him. He doesn't seem the type to age radically. There's almost nothing to him. He's small, thin, spare, wiry –'

– 'Indolent, lazy, languorous, catlike, reptilian . . . he's heard it all in his time.'

The viola-tone was there again, oak-smooth, discreet, but there none the less. Vaguely, loyally, Ian felt sympathy, nodded in agreement and commiseration and said:

– 'If you know him so well, you can imagine the house too. Big, remote, full of light and glass and whiteness. He's got hundreds of books. Even the front room, which is now my office, which he never used before I started work there, has a case packed with books of poetry. There's a veranda, which you can reach from the living-room, which looks on to a massive garden, a long lawn with paths leading even further back into shadow at the end –'

– 'Don't tell me. I don't want to hear it.'

Ian trailed off, aware that he drank rarely, and that Will was sober, and that he was looking at him, black-eyed, liquid-eyed like a seal, saying:

– 'Be careful of Juliane.'

The film-maker paused, then added:

– 'Don't tell him I asked about him.'

He paused again, controlling it, lowered his voice, set his shoulders back, said brightly:

– 'I've been seeing Pale a lot recently, in between film work. We get on, in an odd way. It's impossible to tell what she's thinking, we haven't really got much to say to each other. I've started dreaming about her, which hasn't happened to me in years . . .'

Now three tired women sat in the pub; the one with the nylon jacket and the shopping bags had been replaced by an older trio, raincoated, all with pink-painted loose mouths and cackling laughs, each drinking white wine, talking about 'Your Rob' and 'My Darren' and 'Her Jeremy'. Two men in their late twenties were perched uncomfortably on a love-seat, staring dully at their pints of beer: one was a skinhead, unexpectedly pretty, with small dirty-white limbs in a black sweatshirt, jeans, muddy trainers and dirt-edged coat; the other, his face thin and lion-coloured, was also beautiful, with tightly-curling gold-brown hair, a delicate neck and long-fingered hands, black-booted in a black tracksuit. Two more couples had arrived to join the spaniel-haired duo in the corner: one pair, young, had bad teeth and long bland hair and wore leather jackets; the other were solid, grimly content, middle-aged, in toad-green thick jumpers and sensible boots. Most people in the pub were saying nothing, mostly sitting turning grey-stained thoughts over and over in their minds.

Ian sat loosely, the studs in the leather back-rest of his chair pressing into his lolling form, his friend's stories of love and women running loosely past like bright water over pebbles in a stream, like a baby's pretty petty laughter, meaningless. He thought, with a sluggish slothful kind of agitation, a dim sense of the hassle of it all, of Sophie and Juliane and Will and the dark Turnpike Lane house and himself, the essential, 'the thing itself'.

Ian and Will closed the door on the Dead Hart, standing in the empty front patio with paper plates and polystyrene boxes and plastic forks clapping and clattering by their feet. The serene black sky, cold air clean and fine like a violin-scream, called for profundity, for memorability. Ian's shaved head, naked white like a golf-ball, unevenly shaped like a lump of unset cement, glowed in the night, his ears turning pansy-blue in the cold. Will turned to him, slanted inky eyes narrowed, like the hooded snake on Juliane's door-knocker, and said:

– 'I'm not jealous of Juliane.'

Ian understood with total clarity for a second, nodded gravely, then half-comprehended, forgot, then giggled, drunk, rubbing his ears. Will watched him. Ian took his hand lightly, two types of beauty, hard and angular or strong and warm-wide, and said:

– 'Good luck with the girl. Pale. Beautiful name. And Electra.'

– 'Good luck with Sophie. I hope it works out. I'll call you.'

– 'When you have time.'

Things were happening in their lives, pushing their friendship to one side. The peripheral, the ephemeral, was moving in, making space, taking shape, and something between the two men was finishing. The non-existent, the low-maintenance, ending had its own poignancy, the bass-rumble of wasted years, of unexplored potential.

five

November rubbed its whitish-grey cheek against the Lodge; clots of shredded leaf and listless drizzle scuttled up the gravel pathway. In the kitchen Juliane sat in black jeans and a lean white jumper, the blinding white of burning magnesium, contemplating the envelope in front of him, which was a stylish self-conscious grey, silver-patched and charcoal-dotted. The letter inside said:

Dear Juliane,

I don't know how to start this. Do you remember me? You must recognize the handwriting. Check the signature. Now what picture's in your head? What memory? Remember my beloved A. S. Byatt (I know you never really saw the attraction but I can't give it up, I keep going back to her) in *Possession*: 'Certain handwriting can turn the stomach, after one, after five, after twenty-five years.' You see. And you might also conclude – knowing you as I do, I know you will conclude – that my thoughts are no longer my own; I speak in quotations. I remember what you used to say: 'Every conversation is a duplicate of another. There's no such thing as an original exchange.' Well, it took me longer to get there, but I'm inclined to agree with you.

Sorry. I'm having a clichéd middle-aged winter-evening candle-lit Introspective Moment. I'm alone with my Thoughts and Fears and Contemplations and frankly, it's killing me.

To be serious, though. My occasional friend Ian Litner told me he was working for you. It must be interesting for all concerned. What are you playing at? I take it you were indirectly responsible for the change in fashion-sense, and that haircut? Really.

It's been a long time. You and I used to be good friends; when you get to our age you're accustomed to people slipping out of your life after a few years, but there are some matches that it'd be a shame to break up. So, I offer the olive branch or perhaps, sometime this week, a few glasses of wine?

So how are you? Or, since it's my letter, and you have no obligation to reply, and since you always said that each person is infinitely self-obsessed, I'll tell you how I am. I am ... tired, bored, ageing, occasionally excited by work though more often exasperated by it, not in love though possibly I could be soon ... Which brings me to a horrible realization and also to another of your favourite sayings of yesteryear: all people are secretly the same.

I'll tell you the basics. I moved into film five years ago. I'm doing quite well. I know people are waiting for me, watching what I'm going to do next: to see if I trip up or not. They've got good reason to, I suppose. Nearly two decades! When we were younger we were so blasé about the media, so love-it-and-leave-it, rightly contemptuous, but here I am, still working in it, still seeing the old crowd. I'm almost past my sell-by date in terms of revolutionary new Art. Can you imagine? A footnote, moulding away, on the shelf, forgotten . . .

I'm two months into working on my latest project. It's going to be called *Electra's Dream* – maybe you can get a few jokes out of that one, Juliane, classy smut was always one of your favourite comedic techniques. It's good, I think, I thought I'd be certain, but I don't know. I'll muddle through and hope for the best. My brain's scrambled. I wake up, go wherever the work's being done and give orders without being aware of what I'm doing. I'm excited about it, yes, but the overriding feeling is one of wanting to finish the little bugger off as soon as possible. Get the money, get the workers, do the job, get it out and let The People decide.

I don't write letters very often. I just wanted to get back in touch. Will you call me? Can I call you? Can we meet? Do you want to? We don't have to meet, I do understand, but a note would be nice, it would be . . . civil.

Until then,

Will Corrin.

November shivered and sighed outside. The composer put the letter in his pocket.

Ian sat at his desk in the front room of the Lodge. It was a Wednesday afternoon, heavy, grey, lethargic. He yawned, raising a forearm to his mouth, looking out of the great window at the unchanging scenery: the walkway's sedate sweep to the front door, the rich crush of trees, like a python's suffocating embrace. He knew, and the composer knew, that he was being paid too much for a non-existent job.

For three weeks Sophie's letter had sat on the desk in his bedroom at the Turnpike Lane house, fist-crunched tightly together into a carnation-bud of shaky blue-inked writing. Each morning it was the first thing that caught his eye, crisp on the table like a tiny iceberg, delicately threatening.

Ian found himself, inescapably, in reality. She would call, she would arrive, she existed. He imagined what life looked like to her; the married sister with peach-furry skin, plum-sweet, nail-gashed, the juice dripping out of it, a warped stone inside, hidden, John. He would try and help.

The Lodge was a relaxing place to work in, having no rules, no politics, no modes of conduct. Ian spent most of the time sitting in his chair daydreaming, watching buff-coloured insects come up and batter the window like giant falling flakes of dead skin. He wondered about his boss, ensconced in the studio at the back of the house, a place Ian had never been, though he imagined it to be dark, cocoon-quiet, the walls and carpeting moth-dusky. A place to concentrate. It was peculiar that Juliane, who was so alone, reminding the bulky skinhead of the Hermit in a Tarot pack, of Conrad's laconic loner

Marlow and Christina Rossetti's bleak first-person verse, should bring with him such intellectual insight, that his humour should be so electric, metallic-magnetic, opium-addictive.

The slim shorter arm of the curly gilt clock on the mantelpiece would caress 1, then 2. Some time mid-afternoon Juliane would walk in and ask Ian if he'd like to join him for some coffee and he would, like an obedient sheepdog, follow the composer down the hallway to the small white table in the kitchen. If it was not too cold, they would sit in the crusty black iron chairs on the stone veranda, whose rough curves were glittery and pitted, like a crumbling cube of sugar; in places it had chipped and dropped away, like a flaking scab.

On this Wednesday afternoon the door of Ian's study opened slowly; Juliane leant against it, wearing a dark blue-bottle-green cotton shirt, mole-brown cardigan and jeans. He smiled his lazy sly smile, cool, like Lewis Carroll's smoking caterpillar crossed with the Mona Lisa. Ian muttered:
– 'Yes? Hi.'
– 'Hi. Coffee?'
There was something furtive in Juliane's eyes, silver-skinned and malevolent, like Ted Hughes's lurking Trout. Ian asked:
– 'Have I done something wrong?'
– 'Of course not. I was just thinking about something. Come on. Let's go on to the veranda.'
Ian got out of his chair, turned on the new answer-machine, which sat and clicked and beeped like a science-fiction pet, and followed Juliane out. He said:
– 'Isn't it a bit cold for that? It's November. There're Christ-

mas decorations on sale all over London. Balmy coffee breaks on country-house verandas isn't exactly what comes to mind.'
– 'I feel like a change. We've spent a week in the kitchen and it's driving me mad. I'm thinking of changing the whole decor.'
– 'To what?'
Juliane's head snapped round, its soda-bright smile maze-complex.
– 'A different shade of white.'
On the veranda were the two gnarled black iron chairs and a black iron table, and two large electric-blue mugs of coffee. The bland long lawn was bordered by sycamores, conifers, ferns, a triple-tier of foliage punctuated by warped wooden benches; at the end of the lawn a narrow paved path led haphazardly further back. Looking more carefully at the edges, Ian noticed that the solid blockade of greenery was indented by a series of semicircular alcoves, inside the nearest of which he saw a columnar stone sundial. Juliane watched him and said:
– 'I take it you're not an outdoors sort of person?'
Ian shrugged.
– 'I was brought up in north London where the outdoors isn't a particularly healthy place to be. And I'm not really sporty.'
He waited, docile and placid, for a summary of the composer's upbringing, a hint. But it wasn't forthcoming; an ambiguous silence, comfortable but expectant, unfurled. The two men looked like different pieces from different chess sets: Ian a heavy wooden Castle on a worn felt base, strong but predictable, Juliane a glittering marble Bishop, troublesome and elegant. Juliane said:
– 'Will wrote to me.'

Something went through Ian's body like a slow circular blade, charring and sticking. He waited, then asked:
– 'What did he write?'
And then added, not a question:
– 'Or shouldn't I ask, since it's private.'
– 'Oh, no. It's fine. It's his film. He's just begun work on it.'
– 'Does he want to meet you?'
– 'I might invite him over here for dinner tomorrow. Or on Friday. It might be nice to catch up. I don't hate him. Maybe I can help him with the film.'

Ian peered up at the sky, its gathering and bunching, like grey netting. He finished his coffee, looking into the green bottom of the mug at the last unreachable oily crescent of drink. He said:
– 'You told me he got in your space last time you knew him. A draining influence.'

Juliane looked up at him stonily and said:
– 'I thought you were his friend.'

The plump juggernaut made an indeterminate gesture, indicating half-truth and complication, and said only:
– 'Do you think he'll ask you to write the score for his film?'
– 'He didn't write anything definite in his letter, but knowing him he'll be casting around for reasons to get in touch with me.'
– 'Are you planning something?'

Juliane emitted a pretentious sinister chuckle, inciting a ripple of mild dislike in Ian, and said:
– 'You know me too well.'

The composer got up suddenly and walked back into the living-room, then out of sight through the door; Ian could hear him in the kitchen, making more coffee. He looked into the garden, grey-fogged and lonely, the overlapping scales of green, the degrees of shade and wetness, the quiverings and rustlings melding and moulding into each other. Sophie would come to him, Will would come to Juliane, the neat quiet blocs and batches of Ian's life would be battered and clobbered and kneaded in together. But there was something pleasurable in the idea that nothing in his life was safe; time would pass, pain would lengthen and deepen and subside; the world kept turning. Eventually all would stop, for you, and then you could slip unseen into the perfect endless calm of . . .

When Juliane returned, Ian asked:

– 'Did he tell you the name of the film?'

Juliane rolled his eyes.

– '*Electra's Dream*. Typical faintly dodgy title, like the name of a dubious science-fiction book. Aspiring to the academic, I suppose. What are his other two called?'

– 'The first one came out about four years ago. It called *To a Young Girl* –'

– 'They get worse and worse, don't they? It's from a favourite poem of his. Mine too, actually, by Yeats. The only poet who wrote about ageing with rage and passion and dignity. So you see why Will likes it. What was the second film called?'

– '*One Dimension*, two and a half years ago.'

Juliane laughed.

– '*One Dimension*. Just like him. At least he knows it. And Electra is his latest obsession.'

– 'This one's his masterpiece, he says. He's been thinking about it for a long time.'

– 'I like the Electra thing, I read it all when I was younger.

Sophocles, Euripides – hated that version, actually, it ends too tritely – Aeschylus. Years and years of schooling just for me to come out and wait twenty years to watch a film about it by somebody who probably hasn't even done the research.'

Ian grimaced solidly.

– 'I'm bad at reading. I thought working at the bookshop would spur me on to great feats of literary consumption but it didn't. Now I just recognize the names of the authors and poets I haven't read.'

– 'When I was at school and university I was obsessive about Greek tragedy. I thought it was all so much more vital and valid than anything that comes out new now. They've dealt with all the big themes already – there's nothing else left for us to contemplate. There was sex and death all over the place, more vividly and pornographically than any of the furtive scribblings or daubings you'll find these days. Magic, mystery, myth, politics, art – all the dinner-party conversation you'll ever need. And everything after that just seems to be finding new angles on old material. It's all a reaction to what's gone before. Which, one imagines, is what Will's doing. But then aren't we all condemned to it? Art's tired, the world's tired, we're all too tired.'

– 'He seems confident.'

– 'He didn't to me, in his letter. He expects to be guided by some great bolt of creative energy, an internal drive for completion. It doesn't work like that. I'm astounded it's taken him so long to realize. You need an incentive: money, recognition, respect, the love of a particular person. I don't know. Maybe he has got a spark of genius. Maybe my memory's wrong. He always had a brain – nobody ever denied that. He

was sexy and pretentious and irritating and shallow. He's not an academic. But he's not stupid either. So we'll wait and see.'
– 'He's scared people will think he can't handle it.'
– 'He's got a right to be. You don't fuck with Electra and Freud and all those touchy-feely hints and implications and undercurrents unless you really know what you're doing, or you're brilliant enough to make people believe in you, even if you don't have a clue. This is his last chance to prove himself. Otherwise it's definitely terminal failure. With his experience he could get a very decent creative but office-bound job and earn a packet. But he's got to have excitement, he's got to have the media world congratulating and praising him, as if they're his parents. But I wouldn't mind helping him, if that's what he wants. You seemed sharp when I told you.'

Ian avoided the implied question, standing up and breaking the invisible static pressure of the arrangement. Throughout the conversation he'd felt as if he was rehearsing on a stage in an empty theatre, the broad morose garden observing the two men with its sober dark look. He took the coffee pot and his own cup back into the kitchen, feeling the warmth of the white house coiling and slipping around him, prising the cold from around the tops of his ears and backs of his hands. Behind him, Juliane had come in, left his cup by the sink and gone through to the living-room, where he dropped on to the sofa.

There were certain external signs that Juliane was thirty-nine: Ian looked at his boss's middle-aged clothes, the soft cardigan and well-made shirt, quality and money and taste and, above all, care. His hair was lush, saliva-soft, tadpole-black, a silk shroud for the skull, but groomed and brilliantly cut, barbered. Juliane was a person who took care of himself. And his behaviour, his manner, was the biggest clue, having in it all shades of meaning, all tendernesses and cruelties and ironies and courtesies but no more hope, no further ambition, just the long serene unchanging flatness of resignation. That was how you could tell.

Later that day Ian sat in the front room of the Lodge idly trying to organize a trip Juliane would be taking to Paris the next year, to oversee a massive performance of his work by the world's most promising young musicians. The gilt clock and the telephone clicked and chimed and buzzed and burred; the sky outside was sliced open at intervals by a single steely sheet of rain; more insects collided with the window; Ian mumbled and murmured into the receiver, his biro whispering and smoothing and dotting; a flickering picture-screen in the back of his head ran blurred images of Will, Sophie, Juliane.

A high wail, tremulous, timorous, sexual, came from the music room. It was the first time Ian had heard Juliane play, although the composer told him he was working out new ideas all the time. The arcing whine hung in the air long after the sweep of the bow across the string. It was a half-hour piece, undulatory and languid. The sounds seemed to turn in on themselves, always returning to the same signature phrase. Ian listened, the biro a centimetre off the page, as high flurries and trills slid over each other or rolled in spirals before being seized again in the music's undertow.

He walked down the hallway, the floorboards glistening like the sticky segments of an earthworm. He walked through the living-room, under the arch, into the music room. Juliane was standing there, bow and violin held by the neck in one hand, the other busy correcting one of the sheets of paper on the stand. There were candles on each of the tall glass tables in the room. The composer said:

– 'Sorry, did I disturb you? I was just trying something out. Maybe one idea out of a dozen really works.'

– 'You're such a liar.'

Juliane raised an eyebrow inquisitively. Ian continued:

– 'Don't say you don't care about music. It might be controlled and clever and . . . architectural, but don't claim not to have passion.'

The composer looked at him, not quizzically or sarcastically or merrily, not with any dramatic contortion of the features, in fact, but the air between them changed for a second, its chemistry, its formation, came together. He smiled a private smile, a concession, and turned back to his corrections. Ian sat down in one of the slug-fat white armchairs. After a while, the composer said:

– 'Were you organizing Paris?'

– 'Vaguely. It's a bit early yet. The woman only half-knew what I was talking about when I mentioned it.'

Making an effort, he said:

– 'You should call Will. He'll be grateful.'

– 'I will. Tonight, probably, or tomorrow. You can go, if you want. If you're finished.'

– 'Thanks. I was about to ask.'

Juliane turned his head and looked at Ian.

– 'Is something wrong?'

– 'I'm expecting a visitor. Family things. I've been on edge for a few days.'

71

– 'I noticed.'

The stained-glass window at the top of the Lodge watched Ian walking down the gravel path, back to the village to get the bus. With a red lonely stare it followed his shaved shark-head and blunt big form powering heavily down, black-coated with a stripe of cobalt wool where it was unbuttoned, black-trousered, in November's stifling bear-hug.

At Turnpike Lane station four Asian kids were messing about. A boy pushed a girl; the second boy pushed the first; the second girl squealed, clutching the arm of the second boy; the first girl whined at the first boy. On the street, two tall black men loping fast past each other suddenly turned, exchanged loud greetings, and carried on walking. In Ali's Burgers a Greek girl wrung the hand of her boyfriend, an English schoolkid with a hostile, closed, spot-speckled face. The local comp. slowly vomited out its charges and they skipped and flapped and tumbled on to the High Street in their untucked uniforms, like scruffy penguins.

In Ian's house the dust made patterns in the air, slowly, sable-brown on a chocolate-brown background: a tulip, a woman's silhouette, an oyster-shape. The front room, with its sparse desk and chair and cadaver-grey curtains; the living-room, with its sagging grey sofa like the folded body of a sleeping Great Dane; the kitchen, and its unknowingly pretty alignment of boxes and packets and tins and things. Ian walked in. The phone rang, cleaving the air.

– 'Ian? It's Sophie.'

Silence, then:

– 'You got my letter?'

– 'Yes. Sophie. Hi.'

– 'I'm calling from home. John hasn't come home yet.'

Silence, then Ian said:

– 'How are you?'

– 'Unhappy.'

There was a dry laugh, then she continued:

– 'The usual.'

– 'Everyone's unhappy. Everyone's trapped. Is John being bad to you?'

– 'I wrote it all in the letter –'

– 'Sorry. I did read it.'

– 'John and I have talked. I can come and see you for a while. I said you were having trouble with your job.'

Silence, then Ian said:

– 'I work for a composer now. It's a small job, but stable.'

– 'Is that where you've been all day?'

– 'Have you been calling?'

– 'A few times.'

Silence, then Ian said:

– 'People almost never call.'

– 'Well. Can I see you? I thought – I mean, I told John – I'd come in two weeks' time. I thought I'd stay until just before Christmas. I'm sorry . . .'

– 'You'll be gone by Christmas?'

– 'Yes. I'll try to be. I did tell John I would be.'

The house waited, the air in the hallway and the bedroom and kitchen still. Outside there started up a plaintive howl, phlegm-specked and pained and caught: the wind, children, traffic, footsteps, fights, rain. North London squeezed tight.

*

73

Pale's father, the benign mannequin, skin as smooth as poly-thene, hair soft as nylon, played a small role in the dramas of the dolls' house. When Pale spent hours on the phone late at night, he merely warned her that she had school the next morning, and needed sleep; when she talked about the possi-bility of meeting with 'a friend' the coming weekend, he just nodded and told her to take care. He went to work, he came home, he sat reading in his chair downstairs, unscrambling the long passages in his head, watchful and unseen, 'high and solitary and most stern'.

Pale and her friend Holly sat on overripe orange armchairs in the overheated common room at school, lethargic and depressed after a surprise history test. Holly had freckled skin and rabbity red eyes and a long, straight ginger ponytail. The back of her navy-blue school jumper was always coated with moulted hair. She sifted through her file, checking to see which questions she had answered correctly. Pale ate a Mars bar, prising each chocolate side apart and winding the dropping threads of caramel around her finger. She said:

– 'Are you going to start revising for the GCSEs soon?'

The greasy tangerine ponytail slapped round into her face; Holly made a negative sound mixed with a groan of tiredness and a grimace of pure fear.

– 'I'm going to fail every exam I take this summer.'

– 'That's what everyone says, but we come out top-ten in the league tables every year.'

– 'Except for the obligatory two students who fail utterly and drag the year average down.'

Pale and Holly giggled gently, chocolate-packed, girlie. Holly settled into her armchair, one nail-bitten red hand pulling out bobbles and clots of foam from a gash in the seat; the common room was spattered with fifth-formers lolling and talking and grazing on chocolate and crisps, drinking coffee after coffee. Middle age started here; the worries about weight, the tortuous affairs, authority, the continuous struggle to stay awake. The gingery girl said:

– 'Are you still seeing that bloke?'

Pale nodded.

– 'Will.'

Holly nodded.

– 'How old is he again?'

– 'Thirty-eight. If you believe him.'

Holly nodded comfortably. They took it in their stride.

– 'He's not very clever?'

Pale shook her head.

– 'He might be more experienced than I am. But I'm more intelligent. The moment he opens his mouth is the beginning of the end.'

– 'Does he know you're more intelligent than he is?'

Pale sucked the inside out of her chocolate.

– 'If he does, he doesn't admit it to himself. He's slept with hundreds of females and he'll sleep with me too.'

– 'You're underage.'

– 'So are you.'

– 'Do you mind?'

Pale shrugged, balancing the last soggy-smooth inch of her chocolate on the fingertips of both hands.

– 'It doesn't matter. It doesn't make a difference to anything.'

The two girls went to the vending machine at the other end of the room, wading through crackling sparkling packets of

Wotsits and Quavers and Hula Hoops and the mangled plastic wrappers of Aeros and Twixes and Boosts, saying Hi to people and stepping over navy-trousered legs, navy wool backs, brushing against dozens of female heads with hair pulled and held with a thousand-coloured scrunchies. Pale and Holly talked about Will, and about Holly's boyfriend Avi, who was quiet and Indian and into art and chemistry but nothing else; Pale bought Holly a KitKat; Holly bought Pale a tube of Cherry Drops; the simple–complex, quiet–showy, jealous–loving diversions and tracks and well-trampled paths of friendship ran on into the distance, unseen, reliable.

six

– 'Hello?'

– 'Hi, Pale?'

– 'Will, I was just thinking about you . . .'

– 'Sorry I haven't called. Anyway –'

– 'How are you?'

– 'Fine. Working. You know. What are you doing this weekend? Can you come and see me on Sunday? I mean, would you like to?'

She heard his tone of voice and understood. She lay on her bed trying to read her Shakespeare, feeling the Friday-evening tiredness inching up her calves, listening as people returned to the Ruislip street from the office: cars growled into driveways, alarms pipped, keys crunched and clashed in front doors. She said:

– 'How about Sunday evening?'

– 'Afternoon would be better for me. At three?'
– 'Two?'
– 'OK.'
– 'Shall I bring anything?'
– 'Just yourself.'
– 'See you, then.'
– 'Bye.'

She lay on the bed, the receiver still in her hand, listening to the silence. She thought of *Measure for Measure*, tried to draw parallels, decided that Will wasn't cold-blooded Angelo nor she masochistic Isabella; the silence welled and dripped.

Sunday morning burst out of the darkness like an eagle on a bloodhunt, silver-black and moody. The Ruislip street, pushed to the edge of London and nosing into the countryside, slept late. Pale told her father she was going out to meet a friend in the afternoon. At the weekends he sat in his chair reading or working; sometimes he would go for long drives, rematerializing after four or five hours. She caught glimmers and glints and hints of him around the house, but little more.

She said goodbye to him as she left, and he looked at her from his chair as she stood in the gold-grey dusty frame of the doorway, a look that was clotted and etched with a hundred secret meanings, at once indifferent and involved, as she stood, eyebrow raised in the typical child's expression of lying nonchalance, in dark brown velvet trousers and a jumper the colour of burning kerosene.

Pale didn't like colour. She sat on the tube, jerking and jolted and spitting, clattering into the city, watching her two-edged reflection quivering and shimmying in the window opposite.

78

Her jumper, which was woolly and itchy-new and bought on Holly's advice, glared and pulsed under her chin; where it had reminded her father of flames and rage and heat, its pure bright basic colour made her think sadly of childhood – the glossy depthlessness of tiny wellies, little tubs of thick poster paint, dinky solid plastic toys. She felt best in river-colours, murky drowned slippery hues, not the peculiar sky-light shades of minerals nor the rich thick stain of vegetables nor the effervescent delicate colours of gardens. The orange jumper steamed and stormed and raged in the reflection.

She was on her way to see Will, her boyfriend, her man, half-famous film-maker and intellectual bimbo. She knew she was doing it and sat patiently, holding her black jacket closed, her thoughts as richly moving and fast and dense as a hurricane, circling round nothing.

He opened the door to the white flat, which was clean and dull in the grey afternoon light; where Sunday in Ruislip was mellow and sweet-slow, in Will's life it was tense and harassed, remembering the problems of the previous days, keen to press home new victories the next week, incapable of relaxation. He was wearing black jeans and a dense jade-green cotton shirt. He gave her a general, vague smile and said:
– 'How are you? You look nice. How's school?'
– 'Fine, thanks, fine. You?'
He shrugged.
– 'Can't complain.'
There was a pause. He looked at her. She said, not a question:
– 'So.'
He led her into the living-room by the wrist, taking her bag

and putting it in a corner of the hallway. He hung her coat on one of the hooks by the front door. She followed him into the kitchen area and sat on one of the chairs by the table, watching as he made her some tea, pouring it into a squat yellow mug with a fine line of gold around its rim. She coughed; he cleared his throat; there was nothing to say. He sat down opposite her with his mug of tea, dark red with a gold rim; she gave him a brisk smile, iron-jawed, and they both drank. The room darkened suddenly; a car sounded its horn outside the window. Inside her head the silence was still there, cool and expectant. In the flat above, someone was watching horse-racing on television.

She put down her mug. Will came round to her side of the table. Kneeling down in front of her, he leant forward and brushed her cheek with his lips. The person in the flat above had turned off the television. Will stood up abruptly, holding her elbow tightly, so that she should stand also. He transferred his grip to her wrist and led her down the short corridor.

The bedroom was small and square and empty. The blind was pulled half down the window. The walls, carpet and bedsheets were white and later she would remember nothing of this except the blankness. They stood at opposite ends of the room and undressed. Pale looked out of the window for a second but beyond it was blurred, rain-flecked, brown and grey and stony.

He told her what to do, how to lie down. The silence came in pelts and gusts and waves, rolling in the room and inside her head, because there was nothing to say. She felt herself ripping wide open, closed her eyes, she must be in halves by now, she thought. There were all types of pain in this pain, the one quick stabbing tear, the booming roiling endless thud, the contracting occasional thunder-streak. She understood. The covers had moved off them. She opened her eyes, seeing and not seeing him, noticing strawberry-red ruby-bright blood streaked on the sheet, a short quivering slash of colour.

It finished; the naked unblind half of the window was now a tortoiseshell rectangle of different darks and the room was muddy-aired, musky-smelling, the scent and night and mood coming together in that colour, the in-between ambiguous blue/black/brown of dusk.

Will shifted himself to the other side of the bed. Pale got up; he turned to face her; she indicated the bathroom. He smiled and closed his eyes. Like a piece of cheese on a white bread sandwich, she thought, unable to help herself, as she looked at him lying there. She walked into the bathroom but didn't turn the light on. She sat down on the closed toilet seat with her legs crossed, waiting to see if more pain would come. Reaching to rest her elbow on the side of the sink, she put her forehead into the crook of her arm, listening finally to the blood in her temples, gulping and limping around her body, which was no longer completely hers, neither the blood nor the body. Something had left her, and she had left something.

She saw he was asleep, his body half-bare. She dressed and left, back to being a quiet hard capable doll, straightening and neatening and moving as smoothly and quietly as petrol running down glass. She went home, unplugged the phone and went to bed, sleeping through the alarm on Monday morning. Her father had left for work without waking her. It was raining when she woke up. She wrote two stricken lines

in her diary before calling the GP and making an appointment
to get the morning-after pill.

> Even so distant, I can taste the grief,
> Bitter and sharp with stalks, he made you gulp.
> The sun's occasional print, the brisk brief
> Worry of wheels along the street outside
> Where bridal London bows the other way,
> And light, unanswerable and tall and wide,
> Forbids the scar to heal, and drives
> Shame out of hiding. All the unhurried day
> Your mind lay open like a drawer of knives.
>
> Slums, years, have buried you. I would not dare
> Console you if I could. What can be said,
> Except that suffering is exact, but where
> Desire takes charge, readings will grow erratic?
> For you could hardly care
> That you were less deceived, out on that bed,
> Than he was, stumbling up the breathless stair
> To burst into fulfilment's desolate attic.

The yellowing slab of *Philip Larkin: Collected Poems* lay
open on the oak expanse of the school library table, which
was double-scrawled and picked grain-naked by two hundred
years of students. Pale had finished reading the poem, 'Deceptions', and sat with one hand over her closing eyes, navy
wool-covered shoulders pointed in a fixed half-shrug like a
mangled coathanger. It was the Thursday after she slept with
Will, and she was trying to write an essay on 'Larkin, love
and sex: is he sentimental?' for tomorrow morning.

The library was solemn and old and impressive, electrified by the pupils bent over fans of open books, nervously carving into their Jumbo Student Jotter Pads or underlining passages or checking indexes. There had been a moment in her English class, only about a year ago, when Pale had realized, said to herself, and in saying so saw her future newly clear as a flare in a void: I can understand the leaping power of words, the intellect of syntax, the science of poetry.

But now she was sleepy, writing a bad essay, behind on all her work and having to sacrifice her afternoon shopping for it, carelessly cross-referencing Wordsworth (sentimentality) with Donne (mawkish sensuality) and, wildly, hacked-up bits and snitches and swatches of Shakespeare (love). She needed to fill four sides of paper, wanted in the end simply to write what every GCSE student knew, and every GCSE teacher knew: 'The conclusion to this essay is ambiguous. Is Larkin sentimental? Sometimes, not always. Is he bleak? Sometimes, not always. Is he satirical? Sometimes, not always.'

She was beginning, she realized, not to care. Two anthologies, one a musty and apologetic blue with gold lettering and the other a chirpy unnatural grass-green doorstop with a segment of Klimt's 'The Kiss' on the cover, were open next to the Collected Poems. She leafed through the latter looking for a quote, any quote, to back up her argument; she needed something about regret, a post-coital stanza, slightly witty if possible, to place alongside Larkin's wry 'Talking in Bed'. She found it, halfway down Yeats' 'Solomon and the Witch':

And when at last that murder's over
Maybe the bride-bed brings despair,
For each an imagined image brings
And finds a real image there.

She could have cried or set her shoulders shaking or something; she expected to, and every film she'd seen, and most books
she'd read led her to believe she should, because even Lolita had
started to cry, eventually; Yeats had brought down point-blank
what all writers were trying to find. She sat at the table and
looked at the four lines of absolute truth, but what hurtled to
the front of her head, clicked momentarily in her bones, was not
the upsurge and swell of feminine despair or sadness, particularly, but a cool fast action-replay, geometrically hard and real,
and a few seconds of empty film where she had blacked out.
Sunday bloody Sunday, she wanted to prise cleanly and chisel
and slice it out of history, like slicing meat off bones, make it
unreality, a non-event. She fucked him, she went to the doctor.
One sterile act had followed another.

A bell rang. Four o'clock? She looked down at the half-
finished essay, the mid-way changeover from blue biro to black,
the way the letters first slanted to the right then the left, the disre-
gard for quotation marks and apostrophes. She walked out of
the library, down the greige lino stairs which smelled of disinfec-
tant, into the toilets next to the common room where the girls
in her year jostled for space in front of the mirrors. She bumped
into Holly by the hand-driers, mechanically pulling a dirty-
bristled brush through her ginger ponytail. She looked at Pale,
squinting through her glasses, and asked:
– 'Problems?'

84

– 'No, not really. Not as such.'
– 'Why weren't you here on Monday, then?'
– 'I was tired. I stayed with Will the afternoon before.'

The brush stopped mid-way down the greased vines of the tangerine ponytail. Holly's face adopted the standard look: half-shocked, expectant, cynical. The two girls walked out, into the cloakroom area, where Holly collected her cherry-red nylon rucksack. She asked:
– 'How did it go?'

They walked down the corridor together. Pale said:
– 'Don't want to talk about it.'
– 'What did you say to him afterwards?'
– 'Nothing.'
– 'Nothing?'
– 'I just left. He was asleep. And there was nothing to say anyway. He hasn't called.'
– 'And you're not going to call either?'

Pale shrugged.
– 'What have I got to say to him?'
– 'You've been preoccupied for the last three days. Don't pretend not to care. I walked straight past you on Tuesday and you didn't even see me.'

A little block of silence now sat in her head, born after a fifteen-year pregnancy, a quiet voice which commented and murmured to itself, and sometimes laughed and burbled senselessly: the interior dialogue.

Is Larkin sentimental? Who cares? Pale sat on her bed that evening, nodding asleep then jerking awake, with her essay and pad on her knees and the *Collected Poems*, which she had stolen from the library, hulking in a nest of cream duvet. Her father knocked on the half-open door, edged into the room and sat gingerly at the foot of the bed. She'd seen the other fathers, the doctors and managers and bankers, tired and paunchy and grimly smiling, in bad shirts and too-tight too-short trousers and expensive tasteless suits. She knew their blood flowed sluggishly, groggily, full of tobacco and the after-dinner sherry and the little infidelities with their little secretaries. But her own father, Daddy, she could tell his blood was the blue of a shark's fin, sharp as diamond-drills, teen-agerish. He was wearing black jeans and a black jumper, loose-knitted and slightly shapeless; his longish black-grey hair had been sliced into a shaggy sweep, silkily ruffled, 'tousled', like the magazines said. He looked like the boys at her school, what they wore the days they were allowed to come in without their uniforms. He closed his large white hand over one of her ankles and said:

– 'I've read your diary.'

The quiet new babbling voice in Pale's head emitted a howl which had in it the cry of every betrayed female, the dropping of all the tea-trays in history, the positive pregnancy-test of every BBC family drama series. But he looked calm, he was the same as her, silent and non-reacting, so she just replied:

– 'It was a bad experience.'

His fingers overlapped above the knot of bone at her ankle. She looked at his hand there, its perfectly articulated joints and links and tubes, the combination of artistry and artisanship. It would be beautiful anywhere, some beauty is not just subjective, she thought, the specific becomes the general, the physical the spiritual. He asked:

– 'Are you OK?'
– 'Yeah. Now.'
– 'Are you sure?'
– 'Of course.'
– 'Do you want to talk about it?'
She flopped flat back on the bed, tilting him out of her sight.
– 'Not really. I just had to do some thinking. Don't worry about me.'
– 'But if you did –'
– 'I'd come to you. If I needed help.'

Is Larkin sentimental? Who cares? She heard her father going downstairs. She'd once watched a film, a fourth-rate splattergore flick about the Viet Cong guerrillas in the jungle. Some sequences had been shot using a heat-seeking camera, for effect, and it had added another dimension, as some parts of bodies stood out and others merged with the undergrowth. It reduced everything to flesh and pulp, to organ and organism and the arrangement of living cells. So Pale looked down and imagined, in pepper-red with more uncertain pomegranate-pinkish edges, the imprint of a hand on her ankle. She gritted her teeth and finished her bad essay in twenty-five minutes.

She went downstairs and sat in the free armchair, looked at the television. The room was lit by three small lamps and decorated in the softest shades of brown: soil, clay, the darkest wood. The walls were muted: cream, with undertones of amber, honey, resin. On the edge of her vision her father's face, clean and white as a crescent moon, stared at the TV from its soft embrace of blackish hair. She fidgeted, picked up the newspaper and looked at the headlines, then got up and went into the kitchen saying that she'd make some tea.

A few years ago, she had been able to read and talk on the phone and watch videos downstairs while he worked at the small dining table. Those bridges in behaviour, the past and the present unjoined and not-fitting, made her sad, made her rewrite history, because she knew that the transition could not really have been upsetting; she filled in the blanks falsely. The kitchen was clean and green and yellow and tidy. She was pouring the boiling water into their mugs, also yellow and green and unnaturally studenty, preternaturally young, just like their owner, when he came in. He looked into the fridge, muttering something about not having had a proper dinner. He was saying:

– 'And you haven't eaten anything either, have you? The fridge was exactly the same as I left it yesterday. And you really should start eating breakfast.'

– 'We can order out.'

– 'No, don't worry. I'll make something. I'll be up working late tonight.'

– 'The only thing we can make is a sandwich.'

– 'There's some pasta in a jar somewhere in one of the cupboards. And I'm sure I bought soup at some point last week.'

She pleaded with herself not to laugh as she stood in front of the brewing tea. She poured milk, threw away the tea-bags and handed her father his mug. They looked at each other and she said:

– 'Did you know I'd been seeing him?'

– 'I didn't know his name or what he did until I read your diary.'

– 'Do you mind? Did you mind?'

They went back to their armchairs. He asked:
– 'Why the past tense?'
– 'I think it's finished now.'
He shook his head, a single assured sceptical twist, and she remembered then that he was forty-one and she was fifteen and he had a life that she knew nothing about, had never known anything about. He said:
– 'I don't think it is.'
– 'Why not?'
He shrugged.
– 'It doesn't work like that.'
– 'He's twenty-three years older than me.'
He shrugged again, made another introverted knowing untranslatable gesture, and said:
– 'So what? It makes no difference. Do you care?'
– 'About age? I don't know. It's the first time I've . . .'
She remembered that he was forty-one and she was fifteen and he was in most ways a stranger, a house-mate and no more, and he was beautiful and knew it and knew she knew it. So she didn't say: It's the first time I've read a poem or book or seen a film or play about attraction, or attraction at first sight, that peculiar grinding feeling, the blindness and anger of it, and really understood. And she didn't say: And despite that afternoon, and the pain I'll deliberately never recall, and the images that are now part of a new real private history, I still thought it odd and interesting and unique and, yes, beautiful that two people could plait and coil and shape themselves in such ways.

And even though she didn't say it, he saw her thinking it, and she saw him see her, and the knowledge slipped between them like a slick opaque oval of black oil carried in the clashing tracks of a river. He was saying:

– 'I'm not surprised you chose someone of that age.'

– 'I didn't choose him. I didn't have a choice.'

– 'You know what I mean. And I'm not surprised he chose you.'

She looked at him but he was looking away. Eventually he said:

– 'How did you feel on Sunday evening when you came back?'

– 'Exhausted. That was the predominant thing. I just wanted to sleep.'

– 'The body sometimes does that when it's depressed, or in shock. It shuts itself down. It wakes up when it needs food and then shuts down again. You didn't go to school on Monday?'

She laughed grimly, a too-brief bitter sound.

– 'I stayed at home and ate and slept. But I wasn't upset. More horrified than upset. And I had to go to the doctor.'

– 'You should have been careful.'

– 'I didn't know what to say.'

Ruislip murmured comfortably into its red wine and steak or mineral water and salad or cocoa and the *Telegraph*, safe and stable and unchanging.

Will had seen the mark on his sheets afterwards, and done something that now sickened him, made him nervous of himself, though then he'd had no real thought. He woke up and realized she had gone, feeling the flat's furtive silence, the hanging quietness of an unseen event. And then, like an arrow pointing out through the bedroom door, an indication of escape or speed like tyre-marks on the road after an accident, the line of purplish red blood, which had tasted sweet and tangy and burned on his tongue.

It was a Thursday morning; the air was heavy and smelled of grit, dank and grey like the slap of a bat's wing, slaloming tiredly between the black iron railings which bordered all the houses in Will's street. *Electra's Dream* started filming in a week's time, the first part of it being done in a warehouse in south-east London. A lumpy stretch of grey cloud lumbered lethargically by the window. Will kept losing concentration; he had been at his table preparing final notes for the filming when the phone rang.

– 'Hello?'

– 'Will – it's me.'

– 'Juliane.'

– 'Yeah. Hi.'

– 'You got my letter.'

– 'Evidently.'

– 'Well . . . what have you been doing since we last spoke?'

There was a pause. Juliane laughed; Will immediately felt stupid. The composer said:

– 'Eight years is a long time to go over on the phone. Why don't you come up and see me? Old times and all that. And you can tell me about your new girlfriend and the other two films and beautiful Bloomsbury.'

– 'Have you been talking about me with Ian?'

– 'Of course. What did you expect? But not too much. Just enough to make him feel he belongs. I've got to say, I think your concern for him was quite touching. But we've been working together for five weeks and there's not been any suicide attempts yet. I'd say he's pretty stable.'

– 'You know more about him than I do at the moment. I haven't seen him in weeks. But I want to tell you about my newest film. I might need your help.'

– 'You want me to write the score?'

– 'Maybe. I don't know yet.'

– 'Neither do I. But we can talk. We can solidify past time into concrete history with language.'

– 'Nice phrase. You haven't changed at all.'

– 'Also a true phrase. History has form but the days and days of present time have no parameters of action, and we both know emotion isn't finite. And yet we all talk about our history in such a condensed way, we're so clear and certain of it, its progression. A potted history. Potted and packed and self-sealing and somehow not quite real.'

Will leaned back in his chair.

– 'So?'

– 'So, live for the present, explore all your options and give your history the benefit of the doubt. Ambiguity's a killer but who said complexity wasn't fun?'

– 'You really talk nonsense.'

– 'Intellectual nonsense. People don't understand it but I still don't lose out in their estimation. It makes them feel stupid.'

– 'Which you enjoy.'

– 'Who doesn't? Come and see me and we'll talk more intellectual nonsense, and about your Electra complex. Tomorrow, Friday night, the best week of the night for deep discussion and wine and candles and all of that.'

– 'How do I get up there, seeing as you live in the middle of nowhere?'

– 'Don't be a snob. Train, then bus. Get a pen. Don't worry, I'll make sure you don't get lost.'

Fourteen hours later, at one-thirty a.m., Will lay awake in bed. The shadows on the ceiling and walls never changed; there were no hills or wide driveways from which turning cars could throw a room-illuminating beam. The street led nowhere, was the same on both sides and the same at both ends, brown and slim and tall, criss-crossed by iron railings and sometimes balconies, like a Victorian corset.

Fuck 'em and chuck 'em, right? Who is she, then? Just a screw. Not a girlfriend? 'Course not. Hump 'em and dump 'em. She's the kind of girl teenage boys scribble graffiti about in the toilets. Do you care? Nah. Work, that's it for me. My success.

Will's interior dialogue still had the inarticulate broken-voiced shiftiness of an eighteen-year-old. The real currents of feeling, the cross-hatched doubts and paradoxes and ponderings, were swilling about in some more obscure place, too late for language. Gales of years had pelted down and easily toppled any defences language offered, to justify or filter or explain or encapsulate.

So you're working on the third film? Oh, yeah. Filming starts next week. Nervous? Quietly confident, more like. It's going to be good, I can tell. This could make me, finally. Isn't it – ? You've got to take the risk. There's been a lot of money put into the project but I'm following my instincts. Trust me.

By the time he got to Edgware, last stop, he was the only person in the carriage. He got out, in search of the bus-stop Juliane had directed him to, and then settled down to wait. He saw a pub with poster-scabbed walls, an Indian restaurant with opaque glass in the windows, a phone box whose door had been splintered. Beyond a hundred and fifty yards the view receded into different shades of black: the solid black of a building, its corner clean against the unstable black of one of the trees by the side of the road, the glossy black of a parked car.

On the bus he looked out of the windows but could only see, on both sides, anonymous wide roads under a shifting tarpaulin of oaks. He counted each stop the bus made carefully. Fear of the dark wasn't a childhood thing, he knew, no more than fear of being alone, or fear of punishment or abandonment.

Night closed over him like a hood. He was at a fork in the road, both branches thick-limbed, perforated by the iron-gated mouths of driveways and curving out of sight. Choose the right path, Juliane had laughingly told him.

The Lodge reared up, the red eye in its forehead ablaze; it drew Will in slowly, wading through the dark. He'd thought night in the countryside would pulse with sound, with insects ticking and chirruping, the flaky hiss of leaves and high whine of wind. He hadn't banked on this dense quiet, not so different from the quiet of his flat, charged and massy and expectant. He knocked.

Juliane stood in the doorway looking at the film-maker in his narrow dark blue trousers, black wool coat and soft grey jumper, the floppy shiny brown hair. There could have been a white flame of recognition between them, a spontaneous beat, if not the sense of arrival then some other certainty of opinion. Instead, there was the ambiguity Will hated, when he realized his version of history was obsolete, or unmatched, and that Juliane was something only half known, déjà vu but also maybe pas vu, the gap between the action and the premonitive dream. Juliane's red and white smile opened the bottom half of his face like the knife-slit flank of a caught whale. He was in his reptile clothes, a rippling loose green shirt, slightly shining topaz linen trousers. His eyes caught Will's as the two men appraised each other, serene, lighter and glossier than silver, chipped irises like cut crystal.

The ground floor of the house was lit with candles and, more practically, with low dim lamps. They stood on the glass tables along the hallway, in holders mounted on the walls in the music room and living-room and on the worktop in the kitchen. Will allowed himself to be led inside, saying:
– 'Sorry if I'm late.'
– 'Not scared of the dark, are you?'
– 'Unnerved. Your directions weren't brilliant, you know.'
   Juliane smiled.
– 'The city makes it easy for you to be clueless. Signposts everywhere. Don't you regret that we've lost our instinct for direction? The cavemen had it. What we need is a return to essentiality. The basics of existence.'
   Will, surprised by his own reaction, felt a lizard-blink of irritation. Juliane waved him into the hallway saying:
– 'Actually, fuck that. Welcome to my big, expensive, beautiful house.'
– 'This is amazing.'
   Will walked down the hall, peered up the stairs and looked at the prints on the walls.
– 'I'm jealous.'
– 'Come to the living-room. Sit down.'

Will sat on the low white couch, a blot of dark, impressed and uneasy. He looked out through the locked French windows at the dimly-outlined veranda walls, and then the faceless black of the garden. Some of the books on the shelves in here he recognized from before: the classics, the books on art, names of philosophers on biographies and studies. He called out:
– 'Do you realize you possess the core reading-matter for the whole of Western thought?'

He heard Juliane's answering laugh; the composer came in from the kitchen with two glasses of red wine and said:
– 'You know me. I've always been obsessed with knowing things. Or knowing more than others. Competing. I always feel bad when newspapers' literary supplements publish those lists of essential texts and I see I've missed one.'
– 'Have you ever?'
– 'Joyce's *Finnegans Wake* drives me mad after the fourth page.'
– 'Oh, nobody's really ever got past the fourth page anyway. Anyone who says they finished and enjoyed it is lying.'

Juliane put his glass of wine on the floor and crossed the room to the stereo. He said something which Will didn't catch before the sleek moan of a viola, like a swan launching unruffled into and across water, and the controlled scree of trumpet, filled the space between them. The piece was knife-edge balanced, packed with silences; Will heard only a smattering of percussion, sparrow-tiny darts of bassoon and trombone, a mating-snake sequence of flute and oboe mirroring each other.

In the dead quiet afterwards, during which Will tried to

find something to say, Juliane handed him a CD insert. 'Seven Essays on Silence' in crisp red lettering on a white background, except for a square monochrome picture of the composer in the centre, and some minute red-lettered blurb below: 'One of the best composers around', 'Masterful. A genius', 'Music which is cerebral yet full of passion', 'Someone who truly understands the avant garde', 'Responsible for making classical music popular and relevant', 'The future of classical music'.
– 'Tacky, isn't it? My most recent work. You can tell they're running out of design ideas.'
– 'And the piece you just played?'
– 'The first track.'
– 'I can't think of anything to say.'
– 'Don't worry about it. Yours is probably the best reaction. Better than a crass little compliment. Let me get the rest of the wine.'

Jealousy really is green, thought Will, but scaly and lumbering and cut with black. That's the colour I'm seeing now. For the first time he noticed the column of CDs next to the stereo. Juliane Morgan ten times, he read down, then the vertical of pretentious titles: 'The Head Line' 'The Colour White' 'Next to Godliness' 'Without Experience' . . . He caught the imagery, the thematic constant, immediately, and recalled what had been said in the hallway: essentiality, blankness, sterility or purity, simplicity.
– 'Blankness, sterility or purity, simplicity.'

Will turned at the composer's voice, feeling that familiar-peculiar tambourine-clash in his spine. Juliane was sitting next to him.
– 'I know what you were thinking. And it's not difficult. I

97

compose for myself and my interests have always been the same. Intellectual, but not obscure. Not hard to figure out. But tell me about you – and we've got to finish this bottle before dinner – how's work on the film?'

– 'Fine. Exhausting. Meetings and things. You know. A contribution from you would be good.'

– 'I said I was interested. You know how I work.'

Will nodded.

– 'You're best if nobody bothers you.'

– 'But it's going OK in general?'

– 'Yeah. But it doesn't feel like my masterpiece. I'm doing the work, and it's fine, but I thought I'd know if it was good. Be able to predict its success, see where it was going wrong. You're supposed to have an instinct.'

Julian shrugged and indicated the pile of CDs.

– 'After a while it's just maths. You have a deadline, you have a list of things you want the project to incorporate, you wonder which type of person's going to see or hear or read what you're making. You worry about money. The art is what you take for granted but the success is something you've got to think about. It's business instinct not creative instinct you want. I can understand what you mean, though. The flash of inspiration. The rush. But now, I don't know. Art is a habit, a tendency. You do it without realizing it. Any creative person will tell you that. Art's lost its innocence somewhat. Or its glamour. There's too much of it around.'

The table in the kitchen, whose hard lines were eased by the candles, now had a postbox-red silk cloth over it. Will looked around and said enviously:

– 'You've got everything you need here.'

– 'People always think you need the outside world, or at least the city, to survive happily. It's so untrue. I'm the perfect society man, without the mess of social interaction – books, music, art, a lovely house, brains –'

– 'Looks.'

– 'Those too. I mean, let's not be too modest. We're both pretty damn good-looking . . .'

For a moment, like something snapping alight in the dark, Will saw the two of them in the years when they'd been friends, standing in a different kitchen, laughing at a different joke, but connected like this then nonetheless. Except Juliane now added:

– 'Beauty's a privilege. Your looks have helped you immeasurably. Nobody would tolerate your profession-hopping if you hadn't been so pretty while you did it.'

– 'Well, aren't you wasting your looks, then? Staying here alone?'

– 'I'm not like you. Looks don't mean anything to me. Basic intellect is more my preference. Quiet intelligence. Flashiness irritates me.'

Will had seen Juliane cook Thai, Italian, Indian and French food. Now it seemed he'd added Chinese to his repertoire, unlidding a settlement of blue- and green-patterned china bowls, from tiny shallow dishes for sauces to flat wide platters, like the arrangement of tents in a circus-ground. Will was saying:

– 'This food's amazing.'

– 'I don't normally entertain. I do make an effort.'

The composer looked up at Will.

– 'I really was interested when Ian told me he knew you.'

99

– 'You thought you'd have double the fun at our expense.'
– 'You know me. I can't help it. But actually he and I have got ourselves into a nice routine. I'm helping him uncover the shining beauty of his soul.'

Despite himself, the film-maker laughed. The composer continued:
– 'He's clever and he's getting better-looking. He works hard. He's organized.'
– 'He has no ambition.'
– 'He is a bit . . . rootless, I think he just hasn't decided what he wants. And he says he's got family problems.'

Will nodded.
– 'He told me a bit about it. Probably no more than you know, though. His sister might be coming to stay with them soon. She's had a fight with her husband, or something. I wasn't really listening.'

They continued to eat, in the end almost wearily crunching and sucking and nibbling through each dish. Another empty wine bottle joined the one already by the sink. Will said:
– 'I'm glad I'm here. I don't really have friends. I do socialize, but you can guess what that's like. I'm no different to how you knew me. Part of me wants to have this type of conversation.'
– 'What type?'
– 'About people.'
– 'Dinner-party conversation. Sex, Art, Death, Politics and Religion. The five social discussion points of the middle classes.'

They were back in the living-room, sprawling. Will looked over through the archway which led to the music room, the shaggy white rug, the stereo and bookshelves. His vision doubled, then trebled, then slotted back to one. He heard the composer say, in a voice as distant as the sea heard in conch shells:

– 'Relationships?'

Will repeated the word, paused, then began talking in a monotonous stream-of-consciousness, forgetting the composer, which the composer noticed. He realized he couldn't hear his own voice clearly; it came to him second-hand, slightly soiled, like a lost person calling through acres of woodland, unrecognizable. He was saying:

– 'I don't know. Maybe it'll turn into nothing . . . I met someone in a bookshop a month and a half ago –'

Juliane, who was lying down on his half of the couch, interrupted dreamily.

– 'By chance? Romantic . . .'

– 'Then I bumped into her again at the National Gallery –'

– 'Fate! I love it. This is destiny, this is meant to be –'

– 'And I called her. Or she called me. And we meet up every few days . . .'

Will, thinking about the taste of her blood, looked at the soft pool of the composer's jumper, which was on the floor next to the couch. Juliane raised himself up on his elbows and said:

– 'Have you fucked her yet?'

– 'Sorry. Private.'

Juliane snorted.

– 'When was your private life ever private? That's the best joke I've heard in, well, ten years. Your version of a post-coital cigarette was a series of phonecalls to your nearest and dearest to give a progress report. With graphic details. This is a surprise.'

There was a pause.

– 'You know, men aren't supposed to blush. Well, put it down to drunkenness, and I'll stop mocking you. I am pleased for you. You realize it can't possibly last?'

Will made a noise, guttural and formless, and the composer continued:

– 'I'm not making a prediction. Damnation, hellfire, brimstone. I'm just saying you'd never allow it to last. You prefer the intermediate bit between getting into the rhythm of a relationship and being free. It gives you a sense of excitement. You've never been able to stick living with anyone for more than a year or two, and even then you made a habit of breaking the concrete law of fidelity –'

Will half turned, half lay down, and kicked his old friend.

– 'Show some respect.'

The CD, not one of Juliane's works but a filigree-delicate collection by Budd, Garcia and Lentz, 'Music For 3 Pianos', finished then began again. They listened to the tiny pause between the end of the last track and the opening chords of the first, the scrambled sound as the laser was repositioned. Juliane said:

– 'Sorry. What are the details? I want hard fact. Age, name, address?'

– 'Pale Jesson. She's fifteen –'

– 'Perfect!'

– 'Shut up. I didn't choose for it to be that way. Nabokov got it completely wrong. And so did Freud, probably –'

– 'Even though you'll be perpetrating all of those little-girl myths in your new film?'

Another kick: Juliane's high-pitched giggle. Will said:

– 'She lives in Ruislip.'

– 'She's a suburban girl? Very respectable. Very two-cars semi-detached wife-swapping. No wonder you're having so much fun. Suburbia is the playground of the insane.'

The CD played on and on, its intricate sometime-ferocity muted by the banter of the two men. Some time past midnight, after thirty minutes of cab-calling and persuasion, they were back in the hallway again, and Juliane was helping him on with his coat and joking, and saying finally:

– 'So I'll do the music for your film?'

– 'Come to the warehouse next week. I'll give you all the notes and the script. Come and watch.'

– 'Do I get to meet your lady friend?'

– 'I don't know. Maybe. I told you, maybe it won't work out.'

– 'Pulling back already? I hope it wasn't something I said.'

And Will was saying:

– 'I've had a beautiful evening.'

– 'It was good having you here. We'll speak on the phone in a day or two. Wait and I'll call you.'

And Juliane was saying, his voice quietening behind the closing door, the chipped cobra-knocker smiling wider and wider at Will:

– 'Take care. It'll take you some time to get back into London.'

The minicab smelled of petrol and vomit, chuntling over

and down the gravel walkway in the black. Will opened the window slightly, listening to the red-eyed driver's wrathful silence, and eventually watched the country subside into London's hard lively lights.

seven

The veranda walls were covered in a layer of pale crust, speckled with chips of grey scum and dotted with trapped insects; the patio was slick with ice. Seen from the sterile cube of the kitchen, the garden was a tableau of grey-green trees and bald-spotted lawn hazed over three times a day by a dense fall of rain. In the living-room Juliane was crouched in front of the fireplace, fencing the thicket of red flames up the chimney with a black-ended poker. On the couch, Ian drank coffee and read through the brief letter that Will had sent to the Lodge a few days ago. Juliane turned to him.

– 'You'll be all right while I'm gone?'
– 'Oh, yes. Don't worry. There's not much work to be done.'
– 'Just look after the house. And brace yourself. I'll still have the actual composing to do when I get back. I won't be great company.'

Composer and secretary were both dressed in black, curled like two bass-clefs on a page; the fire bickered loudly with itself as they talked about *Electra's Dream*. Ian said:

– 'You're getting nervous about the filming, aren't you?'

– 'It's a long time since I've done a project like this. Being part of a group of new people. Cosmopolitan, multidisciplinary, nauseatingly versatile. Pulling together and producing something. There's something so twee about it, the way people say what a good time they've had working with you, how you should all stay in touch. The little alliances and allegiances you make while you're there. It's like school. These days it's a lot simpler for me. I get people I've worked with for two decades to come up to the house. We record here, in the studio. If things are dire we go to a bigger place but in general there's no problem.'

He looked through the archway to the music room. Inside his head, something had been cleared away. He could feel its absence, its weightlessness. He didn't tell Ian about the new tiredness, the disconsolate twangs of depression he thought he felt pulling him down all the time, the frustration in front of that little steel music-stand, all those long sighs and head-aches, the hours spent vacantly watching the unchanging white-grey of the garden. He thought about the shelves in the music room, on them the thin faded folder holding the compositions he'd created that year, which were, he knew, simply protracted dis-harmonic rewrites of his earlier work. Where before there had sat at the front of his brain a red-tongued hyena of creative energy which ruled unforgivingly, hysterical and yellow-toothed, now was a drugged earthworm; diminished and passive, it made no demands. His head boomed with emptiness, was electrified by lack of energy. Long-submerged events clattered into his memory, old tunes were plaintively relayed at the back of his mind, ancient recurring nightmares unstuck themselves from the album of past terrors. He'd been saying it for years, for dramatic effect, for his public, as a sound-bite, and now it had happened: everything had begun to look old. Even the sun was no longer the juicy orange-slice of a fresh dawn but the same yellow plastic button that had sagged slowly down the previous night, knocking about dumbly on the horizon.

He said:

– 'I wonder if I can do it. Even the creative stuff.'

He shrugged, and Ian began to origami-fold Will's letter into a spider-shape. Fold, turn, press along the seam, smooth down the edges, adjust the point, turn again. He kept his eyes down; Juliane looked at him there, pleased with his foldings and shapings, and for a moment could imagine what he'd been like as a child. Ian glanced up, breaking the image soundlessly, because his face was recently beautiful, as crisply sharp and fine white as his spider, and his eyes were full of breezy distance.

– 'Sorry. I was in a world of my own for a few minutes there.'

Juliane faltered on.

– 'The guidelines are loose but maybe I can't produce to order. There's still a deadline. And there's the old rivalry as well. Will's working himself into the ground.'

He curled his hand into a fist of mock-pledge.

– 'I have to win.'

Ian gave the token smile of approval and collected the two

empty coffee cups. Juliane watched him go into the kitchen, from where he called:

– 'Pasta?'

– 'Is that the only thing you can cook?'

– 'Are you saying no, then?'

– 'OK. Pasta for lunch again.'

– 'You know you want it.'

The composer, who had mentally dubbed this exchange the Regular Lunchtime Flirt, went in to help. They flitted and pottered about the kitchen; Juliane read something from the front page of the paper; they talked about the garden, and about how many of the plants at the back were dying in the frost. While they were sitting at the table looking into their bowls of pasta like divers contemplating the chlorinated depths of a swimming-pool, Juliane said:

– 'I love this.'

– 'This what?'

– 'The homoerotic subtext of our professional life.'

Out on the lawn each blade of grass stood upright, mummified slowly in layers of solidifying water; at the base of each, and underneath, black-coated beetles and ants slowed and separated and stopped, their tunnels blocked by brown nuggets of soil harder than steel.

November was the ugliest time of year, adolescent, lashing out in all directions so the air bore scratch-marks of black cloud and trees' leaves were ripped away, while the ground received that inevitable freezing kick every morning. The natural world knew Christmas would eventually come, some weeks away now, and would then flood in with night after night of liquorice blackness, like identical cards being shuffled over and over again, winds colder and smoother than fresh bedsheets, a new set of birds to dot and pick about in the garden. But now the naked spines of trees pronged the ground, looking smaller than hairs under the dimpled grey haunch of dark sky. That morning Juliane had found, a foot away from each other on his patio, the small folded bodies of three baby hedgehogs. Stomach up, like tiny overturned velvet pin-cushions, his first response had been laughter. But their eyes had been open, six minute black stares, before a ripple of simple fear made him stamp them into brown-red mash. November suspended the order of the outside.

The train was empty and the air wore the powdery grey mask of Monday evening. On the floor, several lonely separated sheets of newspaper scowled their headlines while one child-sized shoe knocked its red plastic sole against the seats before butting a crumpled lager can into the empty bag of a fast-food chain. It was impossible to think, ensconced in curdled blue seat-fabric impregnated with the city's dead skin cells, fluff, smells. The carriage was full of metallic, electric sounds: a high scream like iron nails across sheets of aluminium; a massive disgruntled canter; the occasional mechanical cough and phew; a wheezy sigh at each station.

Then, out on the streets, there was more noise. No longer within the sliding double-glass capsule of the train carriage, it was as if the top of the skull had been ripped off and all messages to the brain were magnified tenfold: three buses grunted past, the colour of kidney beans and cockroaches and ox-tongue; five boys brayed and jolted each other, mock-fighting, imitating kick-boxing moves, making hand gestures, stalking and loping like stags; an all-night convenience store stood next to the fast-food place, sharing their white lunar glare with the petrol station on the farther bend of the road; four outdated racing-bikes, two of them missing a wheel each, let their crumbling skeletons embrace the rusted verticals of the railings by the kerb.

There were footsteps for eight minutes, the nervous lighter pacings of a woman. With each knock of those scuffed low wooden heels on the pavement the total fear of all the gender could be heard, the anger they directed at the streets for making them feel afraid, the paranoia about what was behind them, what solidity moved between the wafts of shadow to the side, what narrow-eyed powerhouse of masculinity waited ahead. And more than that, and not just for the women, was the loneliness of the city's streets at night, the sadness that comes with each burst of wind, the receding growl of traffic, the thin yellow light breaking out from between the curtains of every front room, the abandoned children's tricycles and dismantled wendy-houses and bags of uncollected rubbish in the front gardens, the black husks of parked cars and lonely brick jut of each roof, each sill, each chimney-box.

The streetlamp outside Ian's house blinked out just as she approached. She tried the bell, whose black plastic casing was fixed on to the door-frame with one strand of grey-furred sellotape, but couldn't hear anything; she knocked on the door, her knuckles clicking like a row of tiny porcelain beads. When he opened it she was ready with her apology – sorry, wrong house, there's been a mistake, I didn't mean to disturb – because the shaven white shark who came out of the dark of the hallway wasn't what she'd been expecting. Her snap-shot-memories were of someone soft and large and vague; she'd imagined his cheeks might be padded out with fistfuls of duck's-feathers and his torso stuffed with foam, his hands would be fatty and round like slices of brie, his voice the useless windy sigh of air through empty locks.

Sophie Brown, married at nineteen, to John. She reminded Ian of the palette and texture of his bookshop days: small brown eyes like commas underlined and smudged underneath with wear, an even narrow mouth always falling partly open like a roughly-handled journal, an overcoat full of browny folds and sags and drooping pockets, like a rumpled newspaper. Her shapeless longish black dress and black velvet choker gave her a slightly out-of-time look; he'd seen chokers like that in shops down the High Street a couple of years ago, and round the fat necks of the Pizzaland girls on Saturday nights. Those scuffed brown ankle-boots, which didn't go with the rest of her outfit, made him think of Victorian kitchen-hands and white-aproned matrons and Little Dorrit. He remembered her letter and its stony anger.

She put her bag – a plump formless leather sack, like the limp body of a seal – down in the hallway and let him lead her into the living-room. She turned to him and shrugged.

– 'Well. Here I am. John wouldn't even look at me this morning.'

– 'Are you tired?'

– 'I could do with some tea. If you don't mind.'

– 'I'll make us both some.'

She went back to her bag as he went into the kitchen, and came in while he was filling the kettle. He felt her behind him, her eyes looking at his bright militant row of economy foods on the worktop. She said:

– 'Thanks. I brought this.'

She was holding a bottle of red wine wrapped in bright green tissue-paper. She gave a queasy laugh.

– 'I was imagining a sort of joyous brother–sister reunion. It's obviously not your sort of thing.'

She added:

– 'My Electra fantasies running away with me again –'

– 'A friend of mine's making a film called *Electra's Dream*.'

Sophie nodded.

– 'I read about it. I didn't realize you knew him.'

She reached past him and turned the light on.

– 'Why do you keep the house so dark?'

Her perfume was a sorbet of lemon, lily and sea-salt, sinking in slow drifts across the kitchen, though when he breathed in more deliberately he got only stale air and Earl Grey; she looked at the shadows under his jaw, at his cheeks, along the eye-socket, and the skin of his scalp with its bright mist of hair. The meagre rectangle of window, with its flaking iron rod twisted out like a broken limb, let in a dim impression of a brick wall with broken glass along its top, a collapsing shed in the back-garden opposite, a regiment of naked trellises to the side, which stood out of the dark like old props on an empty stage. Nearby, Sophie could hear oscillating cries and screams, the type of sound that could cleave whitened shit off pavements. Ian glanced at her, then at the window, and said:

– 'Cats fucking. They do it there every single night.'

Sophie took the two cups of tea and began to follow him out of the kitchen.

– 'Oh, wait. Take some glasses. For the wine. We can drink it later.'

They'd found some candles, presents from Will years ago. Sophie and Ian sat together on the sofa; the wine bottle was half empty. She started saying:
– 'I met him in the summer holidays just after my O-levels. Do you remember? I can't remember my results, but I remember meeting him. I was so flattered. All my friends had men around them all the time.

'He liked sports and cars and nothing else. I couldn't believe he'd dropped out of school to work in a garage, except it was also the sports shop on the High Street and odd jobs in his Dad's office. He didn't care about anything but he wasn't stupid. He always figured that some time in the future, something would come along. I believed it too, for him. He was a survivor.

'I didn't really know much better. Once he was in my life I couldn't contemplate him not being there, and Mum placed no rules on us. You and I were never in school anyway. I never worked.'

She refilled their glasses.
– 'I think the thrill was that I could never predict his moods. He terrorized me and I liked it. He'd turn up at the house unannounced. One day I was too fat, the next day I was too scrawny. Little things. Like chipping away at rock. He wanted me to be at home all the time, waiting for his call.'

Ian knew all this, had been there at the house during those four-times-a-day calls and enraged tiffs. She smiled.
– 'I was so in love with him, I thought he was a god. But I

didn't go to school after that. I'd planned on two more years of it. He said that he'd look after me. I moved in with him and that's when my life finished. Everything I'd ever read faded in my memory. Any talent . . .

'He did let me work, at first. Between the ages of seventeen and nineteen I had dozens of part-time jobs. Twelve to three, minimum wage, no chance of improvement. Every day I'd see the girls from the college, my old schoolfriends, and have to serve them. First they pretended they didn't know me, and then it was as if they really didn't. They just didn't see me.'

– 'You still got married. You could have left.'

– 'I couldn't leave. It doesn't work like that. People always say you have a choice, you always have a choice.'

A mouth-twist of cynicism:

– 'It's not true. I loved him more and more. I thought the humiliation was natural. It was some excitement. It was that kind of relationship.'

– 'That's sick.'

Another twist.

– 'It's always the inexperienced who're idealistic about love. Of course, it went against every ideal of justice, truth and beauty anyone ever invented. But that's the way it was. I thought it was my only chance. Everything is so intense when you're seventeen, eighteen, nineteen. Your world is so small then. He told me what to think.

'And then, here's the irony, after securing himself a wife, he became obsessed with "improving himself", with "climbing the ladder". Took short embarrassing night-courses and found out that he was good with numbers and lists, good at brainlessly processing information. Got an administration job on the council. He really thought he'd made it.

'So I thought it wouldn't matter if I did the same. I could see him thinking to himself that it was the ultimate betrayal. He'd married a sweet submissive girl and she'd turned into an academic brute. Well, hardly. But that's how he saw it. I read everything I could find, then realized how much crap he talked. Talks. I used to read the newspaper from cover to cover, then have to sit through him lecturing me on what he thought he understood from it when he'd scanned the head-lines that morning over breakfast. It makes you sick.

'But that was –' she made a widening-tilting-shrugging ges-ture, and some of the wine spilled from her glass '– years ago. In some ways he's sharper than I am. I'm plugged solely into my own sensations, but he's a watcher. He might not guess the reason but he could tell I was changing. Suddenly I woke up and realized I had no life any more. No room, not even in my head, no –' another gesture, some more wine plashing on to her dress and the sofa '– original thoughts. But there you go. Here I am.'

It was only Monday night, so most of Turnpike Lane was doing its homework or its part-time job, and the older youths were causing trouble in the centre. The eldest came out and walked the streets by the tube station, talking to themselves or commiserating and remembering with each other in clothes which smelled of lavender and old cupboards and Dettol and shoe polish. The dogs were out, too, in every shade of blood-rusted grey or brown, like moulding fur coats thrown over metal frames, blind, black-gummed, unable to taste anything. The cars drove quickly on, women locking all the doors as they approached the junction, men with an elbow leaning against the open window.

Ian was saying:

– 'I'll bring you blankets and sheets from upstairs. Just give me a minute. I have to go to work tomorrow, so I might not be around when you wake.'

– 'I won't mind. I'm tired – I'm actually exhausted. All that talking. It was good.'

She looked at him, a snowflake-melt of appreciation softening in those small brown eyes. The wine bubbled in his veins.

– 'I'll get you those blankets –'

– 'Thanks. And a pillow. I'll be fine.'

Then it was quiet, outside and in. Sophie lay knotted up on the couch, her feet burning under the blankets and her face directly in a jet of cold air from the hallway. She had listened to Ian moving about in his bedroom upstairs, a woman shouting behind the house, the television next door, the hiss and sigh of water-pipes. She rarely drank these days, so now it felt as though red wine was soaking through her brain like cream into sponge, rafting down her arteries and slopping against her organs. She tried lying on her left side, then her right, on her front as if she was having a massage, on her back like a patient in traction.

She held a match to the nearest candle and half sat up, using a cushion on her lap as a desk. The book she dislodged from the bottom of her bag – grabbing a corner and levering balled socks and wedges of folded shirt out of the way – was thick and hardbacked, three-quarters full of measured oval handwriting. She turned to the next clean page:

116

November, past midnight.

I've always been weak; I've never denied it. I wasn't the sports type, always the last to get chosen for teams. John, in bed, was the one to teach me about strength. Funny how violent you can be in certain situations, and how acceptable it is. I was shocked by my own response, the first months. And he was so ugly, so impossible to look at the next morning. People would sneer when they saw him in the streets, because ugliness is always recognizable. But it was nearly embarrassing to be so excited by the amount of physical force he had, how much weaker than him I was. I am. So I've always looked at men and wondered about their strength, wondered what they do with their partners in the private hours after dinner, wonder if they all share that nightly rage which John has. With whom are they angry?

Nevertheless, it surprises me to include my brother in such thoughts. What did I expect? It's been a long time. But he must realize, or other people must see, that he's become, well, is beautiful the right word for a man? John thinks not, would never permit me to call him that, but it seems the truest name for those lines of the body, that colouring. No book will ever do it justice, no photograph will ever capture that glow of the beautiful, the implied purity, the hinted-at virtue. And now Ian has it, though he doesn't seem to realize. When he does, though, I wish to be far from here, far from the explosion of personality and ego. Imagine the mess, imagine the carnage.

Nearly a month to go, before I have to decide. Rage and ambivalence have always contended in my life: at times I could drink down a gallon of petrol and suck on a cigarette lighter and happily burn myself to a heap of ash, though I'd probably have to come back in ghost form and clean the mess up; at other times I potter about, cleaning and wiping, and he phones from the office and apologizes, and I neaten cushions and flatten sheets contentedly for the whole afternoon. Sew a few buttons on to that old shirt, flip through a catalogue, think about killing myself. It's a recurring theme in the novelette of my life, the pamphlet of my existence, the flier of my history. Everyone tries to kill themselves; I've always known that. In school there's the obligatory suicide attempts with sleeping pills, one every two terms, which generally don't work. And everyone knows teenage girls cut themselves, but you never really bleed enough, it's only surface-blood, not the thick stream which carries life away with it. I've thought about it seriously, and I don't have the courage yet. I don't oppose the idea but I prefer to wait. It's like a call from on high. I'll wait until it's the only option and then I'll know I've done the right thing.

Something interesting that I also wonder about: John and I are still… fucking. It would have been 'having sex' but ever since Ian said that word earlier today I've been thinking about it. Fucking. 'Cats fucking'. It seems to fit…

Two weeks. The last time Pale had seen Will was two weeks ago, and now it was midnight on Wednesday and Ruislip turned comfortably and groaned and snored on fat wide mattresses like giant slices of white bread, under cauliflower-folds of heavy duvet. She was in her black tracksuit, her standard home winter-wear, the slightly greasy hair in a ponytail, and the essay title was 'Discuss Larkin's poetic technique in "The Whitsun Weddings"'. She was absently counting the syllables in each verse of the third poem that hour when the phone rang – 'Huge tits and a fissured crotch / Were scored well in' ... thirty-one, thirty-two, no, she'd lost it. She let it ring a few times.

– 'Hello?'

– 'Pale?'

– 'Yes?'

– 'It's Will.'

– 'Oh, hi. I didn't recognize your voice for a second there. I was working. How are you?'

– 'Why haven't you called me?'

She wondered why. There was no reason, any more, she tragically considered, to lie.

– 'I didn't think you wanted me to.'

– 'Why wouldn't I?'

She hated these questions.

– 'I thought you were busy. I didn't want to bother you. You've been working on your film, haven't you?'

She flipped through the slim collection of poems slowly, flexing it in her hand. On the inside front cover was written, in Holly's handwriting, 'Pale & Will, Mrs Will Corrin. Pale Corrin sounds like a new kind of wooden bed-frame! "This four-poster comes in Pine, Mahogany and Pale Corrin! Cheaper than chipboard!"' This always made her snigger, as she did now, which Will thought was a burble of sympathy, and said:

– 'It's been a nightmare – people throwing tantrums everywhere.'

On the inside back cover Holly had written: 'Lost: Childish Innocence. If Anyone Sees This Man Please Alert The Social Services' beside the two appropriate caricatured faces. Will was saying:

– 'You wouldn't believe what actors are like. But it's coming together.'

– 'Have you been meeting lots of new people, then?'

– 'Making a film? Seeing the same people for twelve hours, at least, every day? Oh, come on. It's not how you think it is.'

She hated being told off by him. He always did it, he told her things and explained things and mock-scolded her; at first it had been sweet, and she played the part, complete with demure eyelash-lifts and assenting dips of the head, and a brief spasm of high giggles, but that was – this was her new word for it, her new grouping of time, the latest category – 'before'. Before the incontrovertible fact and reality of their hideous first time. The consummation of their love, the end of their frustration. The premier fuck. The initial screw. But Will was telling her:

– 'Come and see what it's like, if you're so curious.'

– 'Whereabouts? I've got things to do. I've no less work than you.'

– 'I'm sure you'll manage. It's an interesting area. Vibrant, bohemian, etcetera. You'll like it. Loads of artists and photographers rent studios there but we've got this place for just a few weeks. The characters are doing monologues straight to camera. The background doesn't really matter but it's somewhere everything can be set up, and we can relax a bit. It belongs to a friend – I'll give you the address and you can come and see me tomorrow.'

She wasn't going to finish the essay. It was due in on Friday but she was already floppily concave in her chair, yawning like a dog in the sun every few minutes, and Thursday night was now out of the question. She could see herself tomorrow break-time, standing in the Ajaxed Biowashed corridors in the staff area and staring into the heartless black-rimmed eyes of Ms Lawson – who was twenty-five and had a reasonably sexy body with a geriatric cross-hatched face, like all teachers – begging uselessly for an extension. Will said:

– 'And I thought you'd like to meet an old friend of mine, the guy who's working on the music.'

– 'Will I have heard of him?'

– 'It's probably not your sort of thing. He's a classical composer. We used to be close around a decade ago – we only recently got back in touch. He hasn't changed at all . . .'

She carried on with her essay while he talked, soundlessly shifting pages into order, heaving the dictionary off the window-ledge in front of the desk and flipping through it – aggravate, bluster, conceal, deride, elusive, falsify, gangrene – with her left hand, quickly changing the receiver to the other ear and hand, manoeuvring the dropped Thesaurus about the floor with her feet before reaching for it: method, technique, manner, approach.

She stood under the needles of shower-water watching the bathroom fill up with steam. She could feel that the air was thickening with it, her breathing getting shallower; she liked to wait for the room to start spinning before she inched open the window. She flipped the soap from hand to hand, attempted a drop-kick but only ended up hurting herself, wrapped it in a thin flannel and scrubbed her neck and shoulders, the flaking skin on the backs of her arms and elbows. She sat on the edge of the tub out of the shower's range dragging a razor up each shin more times than was necessary and, as always, saw the small domes of blood on her skin's surface, the pain sharpening and quickening when back in water.

She loved her home, with its plushy comfort and distant calm and absences, the no-fighting, the no-visits, the no-friction; she liked the people on the street, who were respectable and older and solid, who re-shingled their driveways every few years and rented beach-homes in America for the summer, and had grandchildren over to visit at the weekends. She didn't like it that What Happened With Will, which she had managed to twist into something between farce and comedy for the benefit of her schoolfriends, still stormed and howled around her brain at home, the way her thoughts kept swerving over to him – because Will had now become the He all women and girls talk about – when she didn't want them to, revving and burning at the kerb of everything she was doing. It makes me feel as though my thoughts aren't my own, she'd told Holly; I don't want him inside my head all the time. Holly had just shrugged and said, 'That's what it's all about.'

She twisted her hair into a towel and slapped moisturizer over herself, emerging slickly from the bathroom, a bulbous alien head on a shiny naked body. Back into the same tracksuit.

Her father sat at the dining-room table bent over the flaking scab of the *Financial Times*; the curtains hadn't been drawn and the floor-length window was a perfect reflective black rectangle, so Pale watched herself approach the vast glass table and put a hand on his shoulder. The laptop's demonic green glow pulsed in front of them, a grid of code, abbreviations, seven-digit figures. He said:

– 'Give me a second. I'll be finished soon. Giving a client some info.'

Info. She wondered if people said that word any longer, whether it had ever been said, wondered if her father spent all his days at the office like that, his feet on the desk, saying things like Info and Data and Let's Hook Up and E-mail Me, flipping through his Filofax. Forty-one, and Will was thirty-nine. He caught her eye reflected greenly on his screen and said:

– 'I'm not bad-looking.'

– 'No.'

– 'I haven't changed much at all, in the last . . . it must be five years. No new lines, no illnesses.'

– 'We've been living the same type of life for eleven years. I don't remember you any different. I expose myself more to the elements than you do. I'll look worse than you, when –'

– 'When you're my age.'

– 'Mm.'

– 'I'm not much older than Will. Only three years.'

– 'Don't think I haven't thought about it.'

– 'He must look like your father when you go out.'

– 'We don't go out in public. We're not on show.'

He shrugged her hand off his shoulder. He stood up and began to fold up his paper, gather the loose sheets and bills and printouts and slot them into his folder; he saved something on the computer, put all his stuff into a pile on the table. He said:

– 'You wanted sex?'

– 'You're the one who read my diary.'

He stepped past her and walked out of the room. She followed him into the hall, turning off the dining-room light as she went, and said:

– 'I only came down to tell you I'm going out tomorrow.'

– 'Where?'

– 'Why?'

– 'Aren't I allowed to ask?'

– 'To see Will making part of his film.'

Something in his face sharpened:

– 'Will you be spending the night?'

She felt as if someone had shot her: there was no air. The dark of the staircase and hall, the white line of the dining table's edge seen through the open doorway, a rhombus of light on the window and the nearby disgruntled hum of the fridge pressed in. She felt his ribs against hers, hipbones fencing with hers, whose arms were whose? A warm mouth pressed on to her neck under the towel. The clock above the coat-rack in the hallway pecked out the seconds, her chest against his, the thoughts wiping out of her brain like air from a punctured tyre.

Later she remembered it as a goodnight hug.

The teachers tortured her on Thursday: one caught her by the changing-rooms, another by the staff corridor, a third beside the vending machine in the common room. She gave herself up to the quaver-voiced commandments of each one, and left each encounter with a new essay title for the weekend. But the pictures in her head were of cameras, coiling ropes and cables, extra-strength black coffee in paper cups, cinema geniuses lounging baseball-hatted in folding chairs, fragile beautiful screen chameleons reciting gilded nuggets of script verbatim.

The place she came to that evening, sitting for an hour in the train thigh-to-thigh with flaking City men, was a concrete badger-run of Diverted Traffic and Stop and T-junction signs, of map-defying alleyways and shortcuts and a silence whose edge was brittle with just-heard traffic and imagined light. It was a black well in the middle of the city, beyond whose high walls Pale knew time and noise must be occurring, but not here, as she walked between the black-chested monolithic studios and warehouses, almost expecting each one to unroll a single dusty glass eye as she passed.

On her bed at home lay her jeans, a pair of black trousers, several T-shirts and shorter skirts, a burgundy wool tunic and slim navy blue jumper, a soft puddle of black undershirts and laddered tights. She'd finally chosen a long medieval-looking blackberry-coloured jersey dress whose sleeves pointed strictly down to her knuckles, making her think dramatically of governesses, paganism, fortune-telling, covens and Morgan le Fay.

She found the warehouse finally, after ten whimpering minutes; the door was a butch metal square whose intercom sounded uselessly, like a bluebottle trapped in a glass. She couldn't hear anything coming from inside and swallowed back a stomach-heave of fear when the door swung open under her weight; for a few seconds she was groping in the colossal empty blank space, the ceiling crossed high with beams and railings, the walls layered with leaning planks and squares of canvas, wood, metal. She dimly saw a gilded oval of people squirming about: a semicircle of cameras and low white staring lights, a young tall man with maize-yellow hair talking to a rumpled Will, twenty or so people creeping about in the dark around them. The blond, the actor she guessed, was staring down at the script in his hand as if he didn't recognize what it was. Will was pacing in front of him, creasing his forehead and moulding the air with his hands, pointing to the script, whose pages the actor turned as if each was heavier than a man-hole cover. We're all tired, Pale could see Will saying, Can't you see we're all tired?

She noticed some things for the first time: nobody would ever estimate Will's age as lower than it was, while the blond actor could be anywhere between twenty and twenty-nine; there were lines round the mouths and eyes of most people there; one woman with a clipboard and rat-brown ponytail was heavily pregnant while another, in more formal clothes, had seated her small son beside a monitor; younger women bobbed and darted in front of her lover; she saw wedding-rings and overhangs of flesh, loose skin on forearms, sagging but-tocks, car-keys left by sensible coats, handbags and a briefcase or two, mobile phones, beepers, pagers. She saw history and experience, so nonchalantly displayed.

A man came out of the darkness at her side and indicating the actor with a nod of his head, said:
– 'Aggravating, isn't he? Apparently he was outstanding at the audition. But stamina's not his strong point, I don't think.'

She tried to look more closely at him.
– 'You must be Juliane.'
– 'He told you about me, then?'
– 'Oh, yes.'
– 'Likewise. Shocking stuff.'

There was a click of getting-on; the fusty particles between them seemed to disperse slightly as they got accustomed to their cold corner. She asked:
– 'Have you been here all day?'
– 'Making notes. The way it's looking, the music's going to take ages to write. But it's a good film. I want to be associated with it.'
– 'Will speaks very highly of you.'
– 'He's talented. The people here adore him.'
– 'I know.'

They walked a little closer, like two insects inching into the centre of a flower. The group of workers there was beginning to break up, gathering in twos and threes to chat. Pale and Juliane turned, she to go to Will, he to cross over and find somewhere to finish his notes. They stepped into each other's path and half-hugged accidentally, and for the first time Pale immediately, automatically, compared the feel of this third body against hers, feeding and moulding into her torso and pelvis with its implied degrees of strength, the hinted-at potential, and she found herself wondering – if she – considered engineering – possibly –

Will folded her into his chest and she smelled wool, black coffee, fresh sweat and his soap; what sensations came to her then were not the anticipated freezing-blue rage or scream-red shame but a cool sympathy, empathy, the slight first benign hush of respect. He didn't say anything about What Happened, and his silence, she suddenly knew, was an acceptance, a forgiveness, an asking for forgiveness, a concession, an admission. He was saying

– 'Shit, Pale. I completely forgot about the time.'

– 'Looks like it. I've been watching you. D'you want me to leave?'

– 'I don't know. I'm going to have to work late on this scene.'

He jerked his head back in the direction of the blond actor, who was swallowing back full throatfuls of coffee and punching numbers into a cellphone.

– 'Aaron isn't really making much effort. I'm going to see what I can screw out of him. Maybe he'll get so angry he actually starts doing some work.'

– 'Shall I leave? I don't mind. I can call you later tonight and we can talk then, if you want.'

– 'Oh, stay. I'll get Juliane to show you around. I take it you already met, back there?'

– 'For a few minutes.'

– 'Didn't you speak with him properly? I'll get someone to find him. Actually, I'll go. Don't move.'

Pale looked at Juliane, who had approached with his notes, coat and bag in hand, and saw her father. Those were the same angles, the same triangular torso, the clock's-hand concentration of feature and manner. Will said to him:

– 'Care to look after Pale for the evening? Unless you want to stay on –'

– ''Course not. I'll be happy to.'

– 'And do look after her.'

– 'You must think I've spent so long away from females I

don't know how to treat them. From the monogamous to the monastic to the eunuchoid. Thanks a bunch.'

Will said to Pale:

– 'I'm really sorry about tonight. The work's just not progressing.'

– 'Don't apologize. It was good seeing you work.'

– 'You were looking forward to coming here, I know.'

– 'It's OK. I'll make up something to boast about to my friends.'

He caught her eye.

– 'I didn't know whether to call you.'

– 'I almost didn't want you to call.'

He put his hand on the join of her shoulder and neck.

– 'Kiss me.'

She tasted coffee, tobacco, felt stubble and dry lips, warmish flesh and his nails in the nape of her neck. He said:

– 'See you.'

– 'I'll call. You don't have to. Let me call.'

– 'I'll wait, then.'

But Juliane's arm was across her back as they walked away, and then their hands were a chain-mail pocket of palms and interwoven fingers as they waited for a cab to take them to the West End, and his wrist was across her knee as they sat there. Then, with a hot crumple of fear, she felt the clotted landslide of her period start.

– 'Juliane?'

He turned to look at her and she slipped marginally away from him along the seat, like the sidestep of a cartoon he's-behind-you burglar.

– 'Yes?'

– 'Where are you – where are we – what are your plans?'
– 'Don't know. I hadn't thought about it, really. Autopilot. A drink? Or shall we go somewhere for dinner?'

She could imagine the maroon slug of blood in her groin, the rusting flakes and ooze. She said:
– 'If it's all right with you, I'll just go home.'
– 'Home? Are you sure?'
– 'I have school tomorrow.'

That fist of pain, the vice-tightening throb at the bottom of her spine had started. She said:
– 'I'm sorry. I'd just planned to say hello to Will. Nothing more than that.'
– 'He was looking forward to your visit. It's not often he involves someone in his life. Don't be fooled by the gloss of media. Or London.'

There was another rush, something blackened her underwear, the punch of hurt in her back desisted for a few seconds. She said:
– 'I'm not fooled by anything. I don't think anything of the media, of Will and the media. Of his world. You've made a mistake about me. Or he's been telling you misleading things.'

He was looking at her in the cab's dark air.
– 'People like Will are lonely. The media's full of people like him.'
– 'So what?'
– 'He buys the myth of true love, love at first sight, the passion that makes people cross continents, eternal adoration, whatever, far more keenly than any teenaged boy you'll meet. Something to pin his hopes on.'

– 'And he does this simply because he works in the media, and lives in London, and the London media's lonely?'

– 'It takes a certain type of person. And not only the media. Everywhere. Everywhere's lonely. There aren't plenty more fish in the sea. You only have a few chances.'

She saw him turn away, to his window, to the endless rolls of grey pavement, the small couples out walking, the blandness of all other cars, the anonymity of other cabs' passengers. It was the same turn of jaw, the same elegant wrists, the suppleness of posture, the waft of smooth hair ... something scratched its nails inside her abdomen, something bellowed at her tailbone, something bared its teeth between her thighs. She asked the cab driver if he could possibly take her up to Ruislip.

Later that night she dreamed, as she always dreamed when she was on her period, of arcing gouts of fresh fluids, rainbows shading from peachy-pink through plum and blackcurrant and raspberry and pomegranate and poisoned-apple red. The phone on the desk next to the bed yowled twice, spitting her out of the dream, leaving her sweating in the lettuce-fold of sheets.

– 'Hello?'

– 'Are you in bed?'

Wide awake now.

– 'Who is this?'

– 'You're in bed, aren't you?'

– 'It's late.'

– 'It's not that late. Midnight-thirty.'

– 'Who is this?'

She could hear his frown of surprise.

131

– 'It's Juliane.'
– 'I wasn't expecting you to call.'
– 'Weren't you?'

Fifteen minutes later, he was saying:
– 'Is the night-time the best place to be yourself? The telephone at night. Or is it easier to play a role because it's late, because you can't see the other person?'
– 'I don't know.'

Twenty-five minutes later, he was saying:
– 'It was good for me to see you tonight. To meet someone new. Different. Someone who exists.'
– 'Something must have happened in your life. Passionate love affairs. Obsession. I know I sound like a teenager. But nobody's a robot.'
– 'I got burned. It happens. End of story.'

Three-quarters of an hour later, he was saying:
– 'At first, I liked Will for the same reason that you do – he had that air of experience, of knowing things, of having travelled and seen stuff. He had some sort of energy. He was the opposite of me.

'We met before he was making films; when he was going through his journalism phase. He'd been reviewing a show I worked on for one of the broadsheets. It wasn't a big budget thing. Avant-garde. Left-field. A lot of interesting, credible people turned up to the party and I mistook Will for one of them. We saw a lot of each other. Bumped into each other at dozens of places. He screwed and screwed. Everything, any-one. Fucking and fucking. It's what he was known for. He got his identity from whoever he was fucking at the time. You had to admire his energy.

'It started off well. Dinners, films, quality time. But people like that are extreme. It's what I was telling you in the cab earlier tonight. Extreme love, extreme hate, extreme isolation. They feel things so keenly. There are no limits on the behaviour of people like that. They have to push things as far as they can, they want the total experience.

'He was always coming to my flat. He'd stay the night and leave his clothes everywhere, dirty towels flung about. And I was getting more successful, I was on a roll. Every new break for me made him more possessive. And pessimistic. It's not the work he wanted to take from me. It was . . . He wanted . . . It was about owning an item of increasing value.

'It was like being strangled slowly. Not dramatic. There was no big fight. I cut him out of my life as soon as I got the chance. Told him I had too much work on. Bought a new place to live. Sold the old one. Changed my phone number. Softly, softly.'

An hour later he asked her:

– 'You lost your virginity to him?'

– 'Yes. Of course.'

– 'Was it painful?'

– 'It was like steel ripping. It was the sound of a felled tree. It hurt, hurt, hurt. No simile could do it justice.'

– 'You bled?'

– 'Like a pig.'

– 'Did he say anything?'

– 'No. But what could he say? He didn't laugh at me.'

– 'Do you regret it?'

She thought about it, and finally said:

– 'Next question.'

– 'Would you do it again?'

– 'I haven't – I can't – I don't know. Next question.'

– 'What were you thinking when he kissed you at the warehouse today?'

– 'Nothing. I could hear the crew talking amongst themselves.'

– 'Did it turn you on?'

– 'It was just a kiss. Three seconds. How can that turn you on?'

He laughed, that sexual soft night-time laugh, and said:

– 'I won't answer that.'

– 'Whereabouts are you?'

– 'In the house? My bedroom.'

– 'Four-poster? Stripped pine? Futon? I have a running joke with my best friend about wooden bed-frames.'

– 'It's a king-sized slab of mattress with a pretty unassuming headboard. Black sheets and duvet. Sounds tacky, I know, but they look brilliant. It's a pretty bare room.'

– 'What did you do when you came home?'

– 'Assembled my notes, vaguely tried to compose a couple of bars. Nothing really worked. It's not flowing, yet. I read a bit, but I was too tired to concentrate. Got some food. Got ready for bed. Called you.'

Pause. He listened to her becoming-brave silence. She asked: 'What're you wearing?'

She heard him move, in the loneliness of the bed, like a fly in the eye-socket of an animal carcass. He said:

– 'Next question.'

eight

Juliane's eyes were moving under their lids, left to right and back again with a hitch in the centre; he looked as if he was trying to escape from his own face. Occasionally he would twitch and clutch in the bed, pull the sheets down, the duvet up, wrench it to one side and then haul it back; he said n – no – da – de – ne – ma –. In the last few weeks he had found three dead birds and the hard red-curled body of a squirrel, and looked a fox in the watery eye for almost a full minute. Every night the sky was coming closer and Hertfordshire got a better look at the underside of its muddy plimsoll.

In his dream, notes were stampeding over dunes of manuscript paper followed by a lumbering chariot of percussion, a drill of woodwind and scattered string lieutenants. The ideas, he knew, were probably there. He had some peripheral fantasies about a viola duet scarlet with foreboding, a springy brass waltz, a love-letter marked with a single clarinet. But the energy it took ... he flipped about the bed like a dying minnow in a salty pool of sweat. His greasy hair spread and shone in the oily dark. He felt like Ozymandias: stone-legged and broken-up with his battered half-face pushed into the sand and the swillback of a mucky sea sidling up to taunt him at every tide.

He couldn't remember the last time he'd done major work, the last big deal he'd secured, with its rushing hilltop sense of well-being, the smell of money. Success was the sweetest get-out route for self-identification, self-justification; when success was manifest and public, bolstered by critical respect and double-tied with cash, with quid and grand and score and flush, lolly and dosh, the language of money, there seemed little else to say. No more words were needed; success made you invincible.

At six o'clock the light began to drip into the bedroom, playing its frigid symphony on his body. He could feel himself coming out of sleep layer by layer, coldly paralysed, until that black stupor became the swarthy red insides of his eyelids. For the first waking minutes he lay until the blood began flowing in his hands and feet, begrudgingly inching along the vessels like packed snow unclogging and becoming mush before water. He reached down and found flannel top, looseish flannel trousers, T-shirt, a sock. The other sock, some way off. At the end of the bed, his underwear. When he was younger he'd frightened and angered his mother, who would come to wake him for school and find him in the bed sleepily naked and blue-grey on winter mornings. It had been his quirk, and in his teenage years he'd coined phrases for it: auto-nudity; sleepstripping.

The Lodge tinkled and chimed with the asthmatic choir of winter draughts, there from the kitchen, the old warping veranda doors, the wide gap beneath the front door and interspersed gaps in the banisters. He was possibly still asleep, he thought, as the room took a turn for a moment when he sat up, and the view from the window slanted hazily out of focus. But he dialled the number anyway.

The white crowbar of morning had wrenched Pale out of sleep also, and she was sitting at the small desk in her father's jumper and leggings working on her psychological portrait of Angelo, due in two and a half hours. That coruscating speed-rush of early adrenalin galloped around her brain as she wrote; every so often her fingers would twitch mid-line and she'd have to haul her concentration back from where it had sailed wide. Her other hand lay in the parting of the Complete Works of Shakespeare, open at Act 1 Scene 3 of *Measure For Measure*:

DUKE: Lord Angelo is precise;
　　　Stands at guard with envy; scarce confesses
　　　That his blood flows . . .

Two sides, two and a half. Thus, to conclude. One may say that while on the one hand . . . although it would be equally true to say . . .

When the phone rang she picked it up before Juliane heard it sound.

– 'Up early, aren't you?'
– 'I had nightmares. Sorry. I called on a whim. Were you asleep?'
– 'No. Just finished working on an essay about Angelo's psyche. Anything to contribute?'
– 'I'm not in the mood. Ask Will.'
– 'What would he know?'

She put her name at the top of the paper, underlined it, worked out yesterday's date and wrote that down too. Underlined carefully. The Collected Works went back on the window-sill, an old Travelcard used as a bookmark poking from its depths like the fin of a shark. She had just got back into bed when he said:

– 'I can't do it.'
– 'Do what?'
– 'The score for Will's thing. Not even the first third of it.'
– 'So drop out.'

I've got bills to pay. I've got a job to do. Money doesn't grow on trees, you know. She'd heard it through her life, through the double-yellow-lined faces of schoolfriends' parents, through the floral waft of teachers' perfume, through the brown veneer of adulthood. You've never worked, how would you know? You children have it on a plate, these days; all set out for you. Never had to try. She'd thought about doing what everyone else in her year had taken up: sweat-frothy Saturday afternoons in shoe-shops, scrubbing down the scum behind ovens in the local bakery, sweeping brittle hair out of the folds of lino in the hairdressers, trawling the streets on a paper round. But she couldn't imagine it, working like that, on her hands and knees in a modern-day version of *The Little Princess.*

Juliane said:

– 'I can't drop out. It doesn't work like that. I just can't do it.'

– 'Have you tried to do the work?'

– 'Of course I've tried. I have to go to the warehouse again today. Less than a week of it left. I just sit, and write monologues in my notebook, and sit, and think, and sit. My whole day consists of sitting and drinking coffee and ... pissing about. Isn't that one of your words? Just pissing about. A pissy job.'

– 'No need to be so spiky about it. Tell Will, then, if you're having so much trouble.'

– 'Forget it. No way. Absolutely out of the question.'

– 'Because you have to win?'

– 'Precisely.'

– 'You're going to the warehouse today?'

– 'Twelve hours of abject boredom underscored by my artistic impotence.'

– 'You can still manage some of the old literary flexibility, I see.'

– 'It happens more when I'm upset, actually. Hiding behind language.'

She didn't want to hear about his work, about the steps and rungs and shortcuts and dead-ended corridors of his professional life; more than anything she didn't want to have to picture him in that wide black bed, sleep crumbling at the corners of his eyes and spit pooling on to the pillow, mustygroined, armpits and feet caked with stale sweat and grit. He's

139

so ... she'd stammered inconclusively to Holly. Different? Otherwordly? Holly had said. That's it, that's it, otherwordly, she'd vigorously agreed, Coke can spuming in her hand on to the orange common-room sofa. The Juliane she preferred was the one that called her at midnight and talked about the Lodge and its surroundings, so she could think of Rochester and Heathcliff and Alec D'Urberville, the tortured effete Birkin, a rain-lashed King Lear on some Herts heath, a cool political Caesar and, yes, her own Angelo. She curled tighter in bed, pushing her father's jumper out of shape with her knees like some giant-chested amputee; in the scratchy navy wool neck she could smell washing powder, her shampoo, her perfume, his aftershave, his deodorant, a hint of his car's interior and, faintly, tobacco.

She said:

– 'How's Will?'

– 'Why?'

– 'Just curious.'

– 'Have you spoken to him?'

– 'Not since the night I met you. I've been trying to catch up on school work. And I've had other things to think about.'

– 'He's fine.'

– 'And?'

– 'And nothing. He's busy.'

– 'Oh, come on. How does he look? Is he tired? How's the film going? Has he said anything to you about his plans for it? Tell me.'

– 'We don't work that closely. I really don't know. Why haven't you called him?'

– 'I don't know –'

The heel of her father's hand pressed down on the discon-
nect button; he took the receiver and put it back in the cradle.
He said:

– 'This is getting ridiculous. You'll have to tell your friends.
Midnight is one thing, but dawn is unacceptable.'

And he said:

– 'Move over. I've got to go to work in an hour and a half.'

– 'Will you give me a lift to the train station? I hate walking
about in this weather.'

– 'If you're ready in time.'

He was curled up behind her, his chest to her back. He
said:

– 'Let's get this off.'

The jumper she'd been wearing dropped on to the carpet,
next to last night's dirty T-shirt, fusty jeans and underwear,
the slips of magazine cuttings and dropped broken biros.
Automatically, she turned round to face him, his hands on
her waist, then her back, then clenched in the hair at the back
of her head; his teeth caught her lower lip, her tongue, her
jaws pushed wide apart; his nails raked her spine and buttocks,
the backs of her thighs. They twisted together, arched backs,
stomach against stomach, ankle-bones and bent knees clashing, one of her legs thrown up over his hipbone, her torso
caught in his arms' strained lock. Against the gloomy screen
of her closed eyes she could picture his strength, not the hot
muscle-stamp of horseflesh but the vicious knots of steel wool,
spikes, barbed wire, iron cables, the crunch of machinery, the
keen slash of knives and the bite of ice.

November

*I have been with Ian for two weeks now, and every day he gets
more frustrated. I've watched him pacing about the hallway,
slapping tea-bags into cups and jabbing them with the spoon,
smashing the dishes about in the sink, wrenching the volume
knob on the new stereo in giant painful sweeps of sound,
swearing at his reflection in the mornings when he can't direct
the blade, hacking at the weeds next to the front door as if they
were threatening to break into the house and steal the TV. He
hates his job; he says he has nothing to do, he says the composer
has nothing to say to him. He feels undervalued.*

*It's the same for all of them, then. I've always thought it, always
suspected it, in the idle hours of my Fulham afternoons, in the
swathes of time when I watch the box and set my mind free.
And I watch the documentaries, the Open University
programmes, the scientific reports. Politics, marriage, jobs,
feminism. All these things are related. Sperm enters the equation
somewhere too, though not in great quantities. All those men. I
haven't found the answer to my question yet: what is it that
makes them so angry?*

*You hear about them, you read it all in women's magazines: Is
Your Man A Workaholic? Does Your Man Have Time For Love?
Men Who Love Their Job Too Much. These days, you read about
them in men's magazines too: Is Your Job Challenging Enough?
How To Work Better. I heard John do it and now Ian does it too.
He pounds about , saying, 'I haven't got anything to do at that
fucking house.' Then he looks at me, as if I owe him the answer,*

an explanation. I know my consolation isn't enough, the dutiful feminine sympathy; he knows I'm not suited to that role. Everything is fucking, in Ian's vocabulary. That fucking house. This fucking job. The fucking train journey. Fucking Christmas. That fucking composer.

I thought John would come up and get me. For the first seven nights of my stay here I was waiting for the sound of that man coming through the city to take me back, like some sort of cartoon lunatic, a tornado-twist of ripping-and-strewing, that's what his anger's like. The kind that nothing survives. That man can destroy things: anything he doesn't like, he breaks; anything obstructing his path he'll tear apart; anything so delicate it seems to mock him he'll smash. Irate bulls will see red rags everywhere. But he hasn't come, he hasn't called, he hasn't written. My address book's there, on the bedside cabinet, splayed apart on its twee little spiral; he knows as well as I do that this visit is more a test than an escape. The letter... well... what I said in it was absolutely exact, but not the whole story: 'very little is true all the time.' Ian isn't protecting his battered sister. I didn't flee in the middle of the night, I arranged a holiday and packed accordingly. I even left John's dinner in the oven.

But this silence! Unexpected. Any woman knows there are different types of silence. There's the silence of waiting, tense-bottomed on the edge of the sofa, mug of coffee primly on the lap; every shadow by the porch is him coming home. The silence of being beaten, which follows the white flash of the slaps or punches themselves, when everything seems to be going in slow motion. The silence of love-making, which is intense and carries far more communication with it than any words either of you can think of, and is never ever comical but sombre and even, sometimes, intimidating. The silence of death, the relieved silence which hovers at the edge of lives like mine, a constant temptation.

It's not John's silence, it's not a warning that he's steaming his way over here as I write, ready to burst down the door and stand heaving in the wreckage before dragging me back to Fulham by my hair. This is a new silence, a new one for me, the silence of the outside world waiting for something to happen. I always had it when I was a teenager, I could always sense tension in the air, the held breath of expectancy and mystery, which other people dismissed as fanciful. They thought I was setting myself up as the mad Cassandra of the modern world.

Things in the house are brighter, though. Those candles we brought out on the first night have been joined by others, and some new lamps I saw on a jaunt the other morning. Nothing drastic: white drapes are always good. And we've taken away those grey curtains; I can't stand to be in the dark. I had that at home. Have that at home. Everything there is slum-coloured. It doesn't matter what original shade, what hue of a shade, what shade of which colour, they eventually turn into something which is green-grey, blue-brown, purple-black, a tone so depressing they couldn't bear to give it a name. It's the colour you imagine everything in prison to be, the colour of the London Dungeons. The colour of a smoker's insides. I left John's house and the moment I arrived here and looked about I thought, I won't be enslaved in this place too. Had to change it.

I saw Ian properly naked for the first time yesterday, standing in the cold lemon cube of the living-room, as I was coming in from the shower to dress. Wanking furiously into one of my shirts – the cleverly-cut bronze top John let me buy for myself a few months ago. The colour of autumn. In my head, now, that scene is still difficult to process, to squeeze through the net of analysis into something pertinent, or comic, or significant. That giant white fist, his expression, one of the arms of the shirt dangling down, the unexpectedness of a naked body in a room. At that moment, though, I didn't have a reaction. Ian just went pounding on and on, that skull-face crinkled up, and I thought about it again, about men: is being male always about injury, about potential injury, about who has hurt you, who you can hurt?

We've gone out. Dinner, three times. A few drinks, though neither of us likes being drunk. Shops, for clothes, and fantasy visits for furniture. Some galleries – my idea. Every week a cheque from J.J. Morgan drops on to the mat. I've asked Ian about it but he just shrugs; he lives in the dark ages of employ-ment, in a draconian time-warp where the paycheque comes in a twee little brown square envelope. Overtime is time-and-a-half. Weekends is double. Work on a bank holiday? You're a millionaire. Ian knows what he is. He's an au pair without the child. A hired help. We've wondered what the second J stands for. Jordan, Jacob, Jonathan, Jonah, Joseph… Judas is Ian's current favourite. His fucking favourite. I think it's probably John. Most men are called John.

We're good together. By the second night, we were arm in arm and that slow serpent of excitement, that I'm-with-a-man feeling, was uncoiling under my ribs. I'm too aware of his body:

the constant shock of seeing the bumps and drops of his cranium so clearly marked out, the flex of muscle in his arms, the shoulder-swing of flat chest under no matter how many layers of cotton or wool, the weight of calf and foot as he pads around in shorts and a T-shirt first thing in the morning. Skin has always interested me, men's skin: that cleanness of line, which tends not to crumple gradually like women's but folds drastically in a two-year period, collapsing into the face like a deflated balloon; the smoothness of men's hands, of the skin on their upper arms and back, the feminine delicacy of a slender, unlined neck. The thought... not of nakedness, nor of being dressed... the dividing-line between the two, the frontier of flesh and cloth, is what interests me: at the collar, the cuffs. You try and imagine the body underneath.

Tonight we ordered pizza and stayed in. Watched TV. Every so often, Ian grumbled about his job. You see people like him all the time. Handsome, straight-looking. But they always leave an impression – of illness, of not-quite-rightness, of somewhere-a-piece-is-missingness. It's coming to the surface now, I can feel it. I'm waiting for that particular flood of phrases to come, and they will come: he will say he feels emasculated, doing the work he does; he'll say that he's being underestimated, taken for a ride, taken advantage of. Whatever phrase he uses, it'll be the same thing. And then, I know, he'll refer to Juliane as that fucking composer, my fucking boss, that fucking prick. And, of course, finally, it'll slip out, throbbing red in a messy afterbirth of post-modern irony, no matter how jokey: he'll say Faggot.

What am I doing? It's far, far past midnight, though the cats

are fucking again. They must love each other very much.
Something behind the house is slamming; it hits against its
hinges with the hollow conk of rusted metal. I can hear a
woman screaming, somewhere.

It was during the earliest days of December that Will had his
first bout of midnight vomiting. He would spend the days in
a frenetic multi-stranded noose of activity, of travelling in
freezing cabs, where he knocked about on the seat like one
black shoe in its box, in trains where he glumly watched his
own face opposite under the piss-yellow lights, on foot like
an erudite scarecrow in a Tim Burton cityscape, of meeting
people whose vents and wafts of CK One, Eden, Samsara,
Hugo Boss, Obsession, Gio and Addiction assaulted his
sinuses, whose pointed lapels and winking cufflinks pranged
his eyes. Then in the evening it was the restaurants, the semi-
social affairs, functions, get-togethers, the soirees. They did
Coast, the Atlantic, Bibendum, Quaglino's, the River Café,
the new nameless Alistair Little place in Ladbroke Grove; they
swelled and purred and drank in Blacks, the Groucho, Soho
House, the Union Club.

And always an hour after having gone to bed he would
lurch up again, not yet feeling bad, sidestep and cross over
from the bed's edge to the far wall to the opposite side of
the doorway, one hand on the corridor outside, the other
pulling open the bathroom door. Hand off the wall, pulling
the cord to turn on the light – sparks of gold, like static,
that blinding white smack. Off again. Then the timeless
classic flop in front of the commode, the bitter heave, the
old fright of being suffocated by his own vomit. The vision

of that cloudy clotted broth swimming back up the tubes, clogging in the nose, some down the air passage, carried along on a silky stream of bile. He could imagine it all, each tiny digested chunk of every mouthful he'd swallowed in the previous fourteen hours; the evocative rising vapours brought on heave after heave of spit-coated mash. What astounded him each time was the babble and sorrow which accompanied it all: the way he'd started pleading to, well, he supposed it was God – I'm so sorry, I'm sorry, make it stop, oh, God, I'll never do it again – and the tears sliding about his face.

There was nothing but cliché for what he felt afterwards, and never before had he so comprehended the raw truthfulness of cliché when he tried to flatten out the stubborn kernels of pain in a notebook: an aching loneliness, a black misery, stark solitude, desolate numbness. Where happiness was simple, was the primary colour of the emotional scale, with the flat bright-ness of vinyl tablecloths and party napkins and kites, the abso-luteness of depression, its gentleness, its sanguine calm was so deep Will couldn't describe it . . . Conrad had got it right, the ultimate maudlin writers' writer, with the compound slimi-ness, darkness, rankness, ugliness and corruptness of his voice, the mixture of all senses, each stretched to its furthest point of tolerance.

It was the last day at the warehouse. A three-day break was next, during which time he planned to try and keep his food down, to sleep dreamlessly while the rest of the city ploughed through the pavement-squashes of every day, knocked back four headache pills at a time, screeched and yowled at their subordinates, stole two hours off afternoon work to finger the suede sleeves of winter coats in Joseph, Armani, Nicole Farhi, Donna Karan.

The warehouse was a block of hard winter light; that flat whiteness was painful to walk about in, and people gingerly packed equipment, coiled up cables, rifled through sheafs of paper, made calls. The marks of tiredness took a long time to fade: there was bad skin, eyeballs netted with blood-vessels, bags and creases, black shadows, nervous tics, many colds; the crew had spent the last few months umbilically connected to the percolator.

Will sat down on one of the plastic chairs by the horseshoe of tables at the back of the warehouse and watched his colleagues moving around; they seemed to bubble in and out of focus; the cement floor was rippling slowly like a fish's gills; noise vaulted about, sometimes coming in through only his right ear, then only his left. He shut his eyes and heard Juliane say:

– 'You've been wearing those clothes all week. Whose funeral is it?'

The composer was packing his material together. He'd been watching Will; old friendship gave him that microscopic view, gave the film-maker that readability. He'd noted the black V-necked jumper, those brushed-cotton black trousers, the rakish boots, as if Byron, the Grim Reaper and Merlin had morphed into one and decided to join Bohemia.

Will replied:

– 'Mine, probably.'

– 'Have you started being sick yet?'

– 'Oh, yeah. I was wondering when that would happen. It's every night now. You?'

– 'No problems yet.'
– 'Sleeping OK?'

Juliane looked down at the tabletop and concentrated on labelling some computer disks. Scene 1. LoveSc. Fight. Concl. He said:
– 'Sure.'
– 'Music OK?'
– 'No problem.'
– 'And how's Ian doing?'
– 'Haven't got a clue. He looks after things while I'm away. Or maybe he doesn't bother any more.'

Juliane remembered a joke from his university days: Two men are in a room. What does one say to the other? Nothing. He asked:
– 'You spoken to Pale?'
– 'She's meant to call me and she hasn't.'
Juliane shrugged.
– 'So telephone her. It's hardly a huge point of pride.'
Will made a don't-know-don't-care face and said:
– 'You?'
– 'Me what?'
– 'What contact have you had with her?'
– 'Don't know what you mean.'
– 'Oh right. I really believe that. How many times have you spoken on the phone?'
– 'A few. Just being friendly. Do you mind?'

Then Juliane heard that sigh; he had a phrase for it, even: the Great Sigh of Universal Sadness. It was the sigh of every person left at the starting-block, each divorced, bereaved, spat-out, put-upon, jilted, held-back, frustrated person. It was the sigh of self-pity and self-flagellation, a windy little outlet of weepy air from high in the lungs. And then there was also the fear, the anger at the rest of the world, the accusing finger pointed outwards, a toddler-tantrum of it's-not-fair, of thinking the world was a nasty place, the it's-out-there-and-it's-coming-to-get-you paranoia. Juliane had been hearing the same conversation in a different bar, a different restaurant every evening, among the men on this project; all the men everywhere were tired all the time, all the men everywhere were being fed upon by the out-there, the something-unseen, a virility-sapper, a confidence-depleter, a performance-inhibitor. Martin Amis Syndrome. So the composer did understand when Will sighed, and raised a trembling narrow hand to the new lines on his forehead, and massaged his temples, and said:

– 'I think about her all the time.'

Juliane shrugged.

– 'It happens.'

– 'I'm going to let it go. I've decided.'

– 'Let it go?'

– 'It could never work.'

– 'You're just going to . . . stop it?'

– 'I've got too much work.'

– 'Masochist. You always play the role of tortured artist.'

– 'But you're not complaining, are you?'

– 'Oh, don't think I don't know you enjoy that too. The idea of giving up your love. The nobility of concession to a rival. You don't get points for that, you know. God isn't sitting on a golden deckchair in the sky working out a score-sheet for your love adventures. It's not like you collect Green Shield stamps and then claim them against the virtue of your soul. Nobody gets a prize for being a martyr. The world's full of people whose inner worlds are booming great chasms of pain and loneliness. This industry in particular, I must say. Something to do with artistic temperament. A tendency towards the melancholy.'

Juliane's laptop went back into its case, the notebooks into their flaps and pockets, the tiny sheets of paper with scribbled phone numbers folded inside the Filofax. He said, as always: – 'You know my big intellectual obsession. I've said it in every interview I've ever done, put it on every press release. How far you can cut down your life, how close to the essentials you can pare down what occurs in your life. The dead wood. Anything that aggravates you, stay away from it. Don't let anything rock the boat. Desire rocks the boat, love fucks things up. Some things are not worth the hassle. At most, they're an interesting diversion. Do you get it? You'll never get to be inside someone else's head. In the end, it's your own version of history that matters. Maybe people weren't meant for extended exposure to others. Stay on your own.'

– 'The internal dialogue?'

– 'That's the one, baby.'

– 'So you're not going to call Pale either? We're all going to do our work and split apart because man was always destined to be alone?'

– 'On the contrary, my too-naive chum.'

One green-jumpered arm into the sleeve of Juliane's long dark wool coat, what he called his Dick Wittington coat, his rogue's coat, with its slender waist and kick at the hem. A

scarf the colour of melted chocolate, wrapped once, loosely.
He said:
– 'I'm calling her as soon as I get home.'
– 'So everything you said just now was –'
– 'I should have warned you. Or you should have known.'
– 'About what?'
– 'My terrible hypocrisy.'

That hem snapped up as he turned round, picked up his
things and walked away under the high arches of yellowy
dust, the sleek longish hair flipping like a black silk flag as he
went. Will absorbed the electric jolt of the insult.

Three months since he'd met her. Only. It made him feel
sad to be walking about the bright crush of Piccadilly Circus,
the haughty greyness of Trafalgar Square and vastly bare Pall
Mall, thinking about the years he'd lived in London and
wondering how such recent history could make the place seem
like a tightening steel trap of recollection. He understood,
now, what made old lovers leave a country of pain, clean a
house whose air had been contaminated with ill-feeling, what
made people burn memorabilia. What made them try and
erase the past.

Back up the stairs of the National Gallery, past couples
in their mid-fifties elegantly out sightseeing, Louis Vuitton
handbags and Hermes scarves carefully arranged, past art students and their interesting hair and space-age trainers.
Through all the rooms, the confusing rat-run of pictures,
honey-coloured floorboards and musty smells, the sleepy
guards on hard chairs, the deep oval leather seats in the middle
of the rooms, like squashed aubergines with arm-rests. The
red room.

In front of a woolly whimsical seascape – lonely lighthouse, twee boat with white triangular sail, woman and child ant-like on a pebbled shore, setting sun combined with swathes of mist – stood Ian with a tall thin woman, like an anglepoise lamp next to a marble column.

– 'Ian! Hi. How's it going?'

A white dart: Ian's hand dropped from the woman's haunch.

– 'Will. How are you?'

– 'Aren't you meant to be at Juliane's?'

– 'Nothing to do there.'

The woman was looking at him with polite interest, curved in towards Ian. Her hand must be on his back, he thought, looking at them together, smoothing under those dark folds of cashmere jumper, that new winter jacket, stroking along the leather belt with its aggressive chunky clasp. Ian said:

– 'Sorry. My sister. Sophie, Will. Will, Sophie.'

The bones in her hand crushed together under their layer of white skin, the knuckles jutting into the warm pads of his palm as they greeted each other. He could see the caution of her clothing, the way she was saying little, the faun-coloured skirt and oakey long cardigan. Grown-up clothes, peculiar quaint ankle-boots. But she looked at him so directly, so clearly, that he found himself studying the calm brown of her irises, the chips of honeycomb gold inside them, as an archer scrutinizes the target. You don't need his protection, you know exactly what you're about, he wanted to say. Ian's arm was now yoked over her neck, the inside of his elbow like a massive furry bolster, and she accepted the gesture, the implied protection.

Ian said:

– 'How's the film going?'

– 'Juliane hasn't told you?'

– 'We haven't spoken properly for a while. Don't see each other.'

– 'It's good. Hard work. You know how it is.'

– 'Do I?'

For the first time Will saw the beginnings of Ian's cynicism, the ugly lip-shrug and hunching of shoulders, the impatient change of weight to the other hip, and recognized that gesture, the jaded pose of waiting, of not-having-received-their-due, of frustrated boredom, from his own colleagues. And it made him sad, just like everything these days.

Ian said:

– 'You don't look well.'

– 'I told you. It's hard. I've not been sleeping well. I've had to give up my private life for work.'

It was a brilliant thing to say: heroic and, Juliane was absolutely right, martyr-like. To have given something up, let it pass, let it slide, let go. It was good for the soul. He looked up, looked around at the talent everywhere, the giant Seurat portrayals of the beau monde, some nervy concentrated still-lifes and loosely sublime landscapes, those slabs of gilt-framed genius, and truly felt like an artist. Ian shrugged.

– 'It probably would have fallen apart in a couple of weeks anyway. Everyone knows you can't hold down a relationship. Right?'

All over London, men were swallowing down their failure like this, with a laugh and slight rueful nod, a well-that's-life shrug. No, Ian and Sophie would rather not have coffee; no,

Ian didn't know what he was doing over the next few days; OK, give him a call, or something. They'd hook up some time. Definitely by the New Year.

The girl in a white dress was still there, still being led to the beheading-block as he walked out, following the signs for the Sainsbury exit. Blindfolded, hands held out for support, with her crimped fair hair falling down over that stiff bodice; the canvas must be twelve feet square, at least. Ian and Sophie walked alongside him for a few moments, before turning off into Painting: 1703–1920. That bitch was saying nothing, leaning her little forehead down on her brother's shoulder.

Ten minutes later, Will was retching and crying in the Gallery toilets.

nine

Autumn term at school was coming to a close; the grey building was permanently damp and cold, the radiators warming
up feebly in the mornings and then breaking down, the water
in the tanks alternately freezing up or bursting the pipes, the
whole place surrounded by rubble-heaps of brownish snow
and sludge. Everyone in the fifth year inhabited that confused
dream-state of last-few-days euphoria, undercut by anxiety
about the mocks after the Christmas break. There were vari-
ous theories going round: read a book and write notes from
memory; test yourself; revise for only two-thirds of a day,
always leaving some hours free for leisure; listen to cassettes
of the syllabus in bed; memorize the book. Pale was sitting in
the common room on Wednesday afternoon, feet crossed on
the sofa, hands around a polystyrene cup of coffee. She was
looking through the magazine she'd found on the floor just

now – Christmas Treats For Your Boy; Sexy Winter Knits; Your Own Guide To The Best Xmas Parties Around; Horoscope Special – when Holly came in, plumped down beside her in a puff of non-regulation cherry-coloured jumper and said:

– 'Bunking Chemistry too?'

Pale nodded:

– 'I forgot about the practical.'

– 'Mocks in three weeks.'

– 'Three weeks and five days, actually.'

– 'Nervous?'

– 'Shitting myself.'

– 'Want to go down and get some chocolate? I'm having a fat day.'

– 'Tell me about it. It's only three and I've had two packs of Chipsticks and a Mars.'

Holly's face froze, hairbrush halfway to her oily ponytail.

– 'Don't look now. We're in trouble.'

Mrs Lovejoy – Valerie Gloria Lovejoy, sweetly – the head of the upper school, was standing in front of them silhouetted against the naked yellow of the common-room striplights. One of her long-fingered multi-ringed hands wound around the end of that interesting chiffon scarf, whose design incorporated autumn leaves, some faded flowers, an angel with a harp, an ankh. Her giant jaunty red-framed glasses were two discs of opaque brightness.

– 'Pale Jesson and Holly Goldman. Are you two not supposed to be somewhere now? Is it Chemistry? I think so.'

Holly's elbow pressed into Pale's side; they stared ahead, saying to themselves, Don't laugh don't laugh God don't laugh. Pale wondered whether it was Exclamation! or Anais Anais or LouLou Blue or Vanilla Fields that simmered around them in a choking stew of synthetic flora. Lovejoy continued: – 'Holly, just go. Make an excuse. Say I had to talk to you about something. And come to my office after school. Pale, Ms Steel wants to see you. Now.'

She hated being in trouble, hated to feel that somewhere black minds were absorbing shockwaves of incriminating thoughts about her, considering condemnation or condolence, flipping her fate from hand to bony-knuckled hand – do we punish her now, or do we let her sweat for a while? – and this school had always been willing to try new methods of inflicting pain: the humiliating one-to-one interviews; the nail-raking boredom of detention; the sadistic clueless school psychologist, whose blue-mascara'd eyes looked on bovinely while you quivered and cried in your seat; the squalor of primary school lunchtime patrol; the snide reports to the board of governors; the child-labour litter-duty. But Ms Steel's asexual office, with its cordy baldy grey carpet and meno-pause-beige walls studded with dusty plaques and photos, and giant skulking oak desk festooned with family pictures of an android husband and three goblin children, and the oval slab of conference-table in the centre of the room, was the final point of the anti-disobedience whistle-stop campaign. Pale stared at Mrs Lovejoy, whose wedding-and-engagement ring duo shone elegantly at her. Lovejoy said:
– 'I said now. Up you get. You're a in a great deal of trouble. A great deal.'

Ms Steel – Josephine Steel; how far was that from Josef Stalin? – was almost invisible in the office. The window was behind her, looking out on to the dripping gravy-brown quad; Pale stumbled forward in the opalescent grey air. She could actually see fat particles of dust floating about reluctantly like drowsy mosquitoes, restricting her movements. It seemed as though gravity had doubled, here in the Head's Office, she was moving so slowly. Square-shouldered and tank-like above the upper-line of the leather chair was the cement-block head of Ms Steel – Pale thought of Big Brother, Mastermind, the Devil, God – and she could work out the pose, brogues planted on the floor like the feet of a stubborn rhino, hands gripping the arm-rests like an electrocuted killer, eyes staring straight ahead like Robocop, like Robocop 2, like the protagonists in all the videos she'd seen: Maniac Cop, Killer Sergeant, The Invalidator, Horrorhead.

– 'Pale Jesson.'

Then:

– 'Mmnn.'

Then:

– 'Pale Jesson. Sit down.'

Inside that voice was trapped the raw-gummed screams of every slapped, caned, buggered, solitary-confined student, the smack of every wooden ruler on every trembling palm. It started before Pale had even reached the spindly wooden chair – straight-backed, no arms – opposite the desk.

– 'I've been talking to your teachers. And the head of the upper school. There's been a letter sent to your father. I'm not happy. Do you know why?'

Silence, then:

– 'Do you know why?'

And finally:

– 'I think you do.'

A sigh bigger deeper and grander than the parting of the Red Sea, with a rattle-shake of phlegm in its tail.

– 'It's not good enough. What do you call it these days? Bunking, cutting class, skiving? It's all the same thing. And we know you do it. Don't think we don't notice.'

The paunchy hands clapped together, slammed on the desk, wound around each other like a Chinese Dragon, danced and plummeted in the air, pulled each other about in a passionate embrace of withered might.

– 'Why do you come to school? Why do you even bother? Would you not find it easier to pursue your extra-curricular interests if you simply stayed at home?'

The fifth-formers had all discussed this method of intimidation before, sitting in a laughing circle in the common room; teachers followed no conceivable form of logic. Their job was simply to make you feel bad. They constructed a retaliatory joke: Knock knock. Who's there? Ms Steel. Fuck off, then. The voice went on; at its highest point it was like the sudden yelp of car-brakes, at its lowest it echoed the bass-growl of an avalanche.

– 'Do you know how much your father has to pay every year for you to attend this school? How many people would love to be in your position? Do you not think it's the highest mark of disrespect to feel you can reject such advantages? We've had our eye on you. And we're far from happy.'

Then, the obligatory damning-with-faint-praise.

– 'You're not unintelligent. The chances of you achieving reasonably good grades at GCSE level aren't remote. You do

161

have some potential. Teachers have put their faith in you. Now . . .'

The business-like closing of the session, the nod towards adult-like equality, the now-we-understand-each-other expansive hand gesture, the softening of tone to something between pus and semen.
– 'You know what we want. We want to see higher grades. A better attendance record. Greater concentration. More respect for the teachers who've done so much work, just for you, more respect for your father for sending you here, more respect for your colleagues. Don't think there's one set of rules for you, and another for everyone else.'

Then the cruel final sentence, the one guaranteed to resound in Pale's head for months afterwards.
– 'You must realize that you are no better than anyone else at this school.'

She wondered how many wrist-slashings Ms Steel had been personally responsible for. Outside, finally, she felt like someone whose senses were recovering after a bout of amnesia. 'In The Head's Office, Nobody Can Hear You Scream', read the green biro on a toilet door upstairs. 'In The Head's Office, You Can't Scream – There Isn't Enough Oxygen', ran the blue-ink reply. She bunked the rest of the afternoon and came home early enough to intercept the letter to her father. She was good at this: tear it into tiny pieces, hold the bits in cupped hands under the tap until pulpy, wrap in toilet paper. Flush away.

The last two days of school were a flash of blu-tacked tinsel, corny cards, late homework and stress. Are you going to revise for the mocks? Isn't it true they make them harder than the real thing? I thought they didn't expect you to work for them – you're meant to be shocked into working for the summer exams because you do so badly. I might flick through the textbooks, but nothing more than that. I thought I'd just memorize an essay. To her, mocks were a mirage, exams were a pixelvision fantasy in the far distance, rippling out of view, unreal, unreliable. The days and nights had passed by like the slick pages of a flipped magazine – an old rubber stamp of words and images, leaving no impression.

Friday came, school was finished until the first week of January, and she launched off into the choppy waters of that evening's television: comedy, of sorts, on all the channels. Everything was turning into comedy, the whole world was laughing: sketches, slapstick, political satire, social satire, ironic chatshows, youth TV, post-modern post-ironic post-feminist drek. Somewhere sounded the dry rumble of fear about the exams – three weeks and two days, now – and she resolved to make a list of things to do, make a timetable from the list, tomorrow, or maybe Monday. But the sofa's soft caramel palm patted her into drowsy televisual watchfulness: she had a mug of tea, half a Galaxy bar, yesterday's pizza, hot chocolate, biscuits. Her insides must be a metropolis of bad health, with rivers of fat bursting their banks against cholesterol shacks and giant sugar skyscrapers. The downstairs phone rang. Holly was due to call, so Pale simply said:

– 'Hey.'

– 'Pale?'

– 'Dad?'

– 'Who were you expecting?'

– 'Holly. Not a man, before you ask. What do you – What's up?'

– 'Listen, someone called me at the office.'

– 'Is something wrong?'

– 'Quite the opposite. He's a guy I used to work with. Invited me up for a conference this weekend. In Manchester.'

She picked the last biscuit out of the tin.

– 'How long'll you be gone?'

– "Til Sunday.'

– 'See you, then.'

She put the phone down on him, wondering about his professional chum, this new mysterious invite. She wondered whether they sat around at conferences like this, all wearing T-shirts saying 'It's a Solicitor Thing – You Wouldn't Understand'. The Cult of Financial Advisers. A secret pow-wow. On the Ruislip cul-de-sac, Volvos and Range Rovers chuckled into driveways, the odd Mercedes slipped out of a garage, an adolescent boy took his birthday-present BMW out for a drive, but mostly people stayed in, listened to the radio, watched TV, caught up with the novels they'd neglected during the working week.

By nine-thirty she was trying to remember what clothes he'd left the house in that morning, wondered whether he'd be on the train up to Manchester, or – no, of course – he'd be in the car. With his friend, who was – what? – smooth, a slinky solicitor like him. The vocabulary for male relationships made it difficult to divine how close they were, had been, could become, and the tone of the male voice was swiftly capable of covering tracks. A guy I used to work with; somebody I once knew; he called me at the office. Did you call chums

guys? Mates chums? Did previous acquaintance mean previous friendship? Are friendly colleagues actually friends?
Buddy, comrade, chum, acquaintance, client, pal, drinking-
mate, mucker . . . she wondered what he was thinking, what
pictures were on the lonely cinema-screen, inside the empty
auditorium of that sleek brain. She'd felt it when she screwed
him, as she had when she screwed Will, as she might with
Juliane: the creeping brown silt of isolation shaking about
inside them, keeping time with everything they did, generally
lost in the scream of everyday living, then occasionally noticed,
then impossible not to follow, like a car-alarm in city traffic.
She knew that many men had it, these days, that mid-life crises
were the new vogue, but it had become her addiction, it gave
her some new trail to follow that wasn't hot-wired just to her
own feelings.

Holly eventually called. Not going out tonight, Hol? No
way; I've started revising. So soon? Well, they are in three
weeks. Three weeks and two days, actually. And they talked
about getting jobs, Holly's boyfriend, the new clothes shop
out on Oxford Street – satin skirts for a tenner, no different
to the ones in Top Shop, which were double the price – and
sat through half an hour of TV comedy together. Pale said:
– 'I'd better get off the phone.'
– 'You're staying in tonight?'
– 'Dad's gone to a conference with some friend of his.'
– 'He just left you there for the weekend?'
– 'I'll be fine. I like it when he's away and I get the house to
myself.'
– 'Oh, because it's so cramped when he's around, right? Don't
you get scared?'

– 'Of being alone? No.'

– 'I get spooked really easily. I can't even stay on my own downstairs. I'm too used to having my sisters around the place making noise.'

Pale looked round the through-lounge, with its serene large shadows, the dining table at the far end, the window. From the kitchen came a series of stiff clicks, a pentatonic scale of water-drops on metal, a wooden creak. The floorboards in the landing and stairs were stretching out against the walls; upstairs was something like a footstep. She said:

– 'Oh, don't start. I'm starting to get nervous now.'

– 'Sorry. Go round the house and turn all the lights on. And keep the radio on when you go to sleep.'

But, of course, the living-room light snapped once in its death-throe and the localized shine of the television once more lit the room. When the conversation with Holly was over she forced herself upstairs, ignoring the prickle of over-your-shoulder terror, brushed her teeth with the landing and bed-room lights on, and the door wide open, got into bed still in her tracksuit bottom and socks. On the radio was a saccharine stream of love songs, then a medley of 1980s chart hits that made her nostalgic for no reason. At midnight – midnight oh three, she was staring at the clock when it happened – the phone rang.

– 'Hello?'

Silence. She ran through the possibilities in her mind: a problem on the line; Will, nervous; Juliane, playing a joke; her father, checking she was still at home. Then the breathing, harsh, a great inhalation of sandpaper and wood-shavings and an exhalation of drizzly air punctuated by a small pause. She crashed the receiver down but it only rang again, and she found herself listening to the breathing, not brave enough to insult him, even afraid of saying the wrong thing. So: a rasping breath, the switch-flick catch in the middle, a strained out-sigh, and the usual questions, the ones she'd heard on the phone before: was she in bed? Alone? What was she wearing? What was she thinking of? And she heard it there too, of course, the snake-hiss of solitude, the eel-shimmy of confusion, the pneumatic drill of London living.

Pervert callers always made her contemplative and, without anger, she would wonder what they had been wearing, where they'd been calling from, what dredged-up longings made them want to speak with her, and with that shortly followed a sense of her own – what? – a sense of her alone-ness. Singularity? Singleness, more like. Apartness.

These days, *The Bell Jar* and *Catcher in the Rye* had pride of place on her window-ledge, next to the Shakespeare and her Larkin collections.

She wanted to find out how he was, so she called him. Perfectly civil. Just a chat: Hey, how's it going? We haven't spoken in a while. Just thought I'd find out how you are, how things are. And how are things? How's work? And later, casually, with no reference to self: So, are you seeing anyone? Seeing anyone; she loved that phrase. Seeing meant fucking. Everyone knew that.

Sleepy.

– 'Yeah?'

– 'Will?'

Three seconds of silence.

– 'Pale?'

The hard loop in her chest loosened.

– 'Will.'

Just to say his name.

'Pale.'

Just to say hers. She said:

– 'I just called to say hi. To see how you're doing.'

– 'I'm doing fine.'

– 'Working?'

A yawn.

– 'Working and puking. Fourteen hours of work equals one throwing-up session ninety minutes later.'

– 'Oh, baby. Don't be ill.'

Oh, baby. She'd never heard that tone in her own voice before, that timbre of regurgitated confectionery: milk chocolate vowels, caramel-creme consonants, angel-delight prepositions. Oh, baby. Don't be ill. Did Holly speak like this to her boyfriend? And Will was talking back like that too, with champagne-truffle questions and maple-syrup comments, as they murmured on, two faceless voices in the chic bitter chocolate Bloomsbury night and the crackling Milk Tray dark of Ruislip.

Soon, sooner than either of them expected, they began talking about the institution of We, the bond of Us, the seemingly separate entity of Our Relationship – grown-up words for grown-up concepts. Without seeing it, they sailed their serene little dinghy into a choppy swell of Issues and Considerations and Priorities and Factors, and then Will was saying:

– 'It's just with the film and everything . . .'

And she was saying:

– 'And after the mocks is when we've really got to start working.'

And he was saying:

– 'Maybe, what, around May?'

And she had to say:

– 'Actually, I think July'll probably be most convenient for me.'

At one oh one she finally said:

– 'Well?'

– 'Well.'

– 'You know, I can't think of anything to say that isn't a cliché.'

– 'It was good talking to you.'

There was respect there, as sweet as crystallized orange slices, sugar-covered almonds, buttermilk, a family box of After Eights.

– 'It was good, it really was. I'm going first. I'm hanging up now.'

Deep breath at the other end of the line. He said:

– 'Bye, now.'

One oh three. And she was left with nothing to think.

– 'Bye.'

The next morning Oxford Street was a paper tunnel of cut-out Reindeer and Santas, with soggy worms of tinsel draped over every lamp-post and most shop windows half-obscured by a wedge of fake snow. By midday it was raining continuously, and there was nothing romantic about it, it dropped down in a grey wash, running dirt-packed alongside the curb and poo-ling in dips in the pavement, plummeting hard off tarpaulin-edges. She bought a topaz jersey dress, a black chiffon tunic, two pairs of leggings to join the confused faded dozen that were already knotted at the bottom of her wardrobe, a party dress in beetroot-coloured satin that she knew she'd never have an opportunity to wear, a pair of peach-soft leather boots, some wide Bambi-brown velvet trousers. In the food department of Marks & Sparks she squeezed in between the big dusty raincoated people, their mock-crocodile briefcases dripping, and picked out some blueberry muffins, ready-made pasta salads, bacon sandwiches, a slab of Belgian chocolate, some single-person microwave meals. She walked through Soho, which was empty and ugly for once, and up round the back of Covent Garden. At Space NK she bought some silver nail polish, lip balm for five pounds, hair serum, moisturiser with sunscreen – you could never be too careful – and some Nearly Nude eyeshadow. At that kooky poky jewellers' she spent too much on a pair of silver cufflinks, a minute heart engraved on each one, and had the day's date put on there as well; before she could stop herself, she asked for them to be packed and sent direct to Will. Nothing more than a token of friendship.

That evening, alone in the house:

– 'Juliane?'

– 'Pale! I wasn't expecting you to call. I thought you had school work. How's it going?'

– 'Fine. Christmas holidays have started now. My Dad's gone away for the weekend. You?'

– 'Working. Or trying to work.'

– 'Can you come out tomorrow night?'

A pause, and then he said:

– 'Has something happened?'
– 'No. Not as such. I called Will last night.'
– 'And?'
– 'We split up, I suppose.'
  He laughed:
– 'You suppose? Well, either you did or you didn't.'
– 'We were never really together to split up, were we?'
  The TV flared into life in the Ruislip sitting-room. Pale waited for his answer, which was:
– 'Let's talk about something else.'
  She took a sip of cappuccino (limp, tired froth; coffee like petrol) and a mouthful of pasta and chicken salad. The Belgian chocolate lay on the magazine-table with its gold wrapper peeling back like sheets on a newly-made bed. Her tracksuit was moistly speckled with crumbs of muffin. She said:
– 'OK. Dinner, tomorrow night. Diversion for both of us.'
– 'What d'you fancy?'
– 'Something I haven't had before. Japanese?'
  Angel tube, then, seven-thirty on Sunday. After the excitement of the phonecall, the success of the conversation, the accepted request for a date, a tête-à-tête, a rendez-vous, a meeting of like minds, she realized she didn't want to go. She went into the kitchen and put her lasagna, in its plastic tray, into the microwave.
  That evening, she dreamed so vividly and lucidly that when she awoke the next morning she thought a whole day had actually passed. She listened to the thick quiet of snow falling on the street outside, the walls in her bedroom pulsing with the whiteness of morning light, and went downstairs to watch TV. She could smell herself: the warm oiliness of her hair,

the mouldy felt of her armpits, the grainy tang of her feet. She'd slept in the same tracksuit for two nights now and hadn't had a shower in the time her father had been away. She didn't feel depressed; she couldn't point out the boundaries of her bad-feeling, the parameters of her neurosis. She ate a Marks sandwich and unloaded another sachet of cappuccino into a mug; she sat in front of the box, the sitting-room curtains still drawn, but she didn't want to have to see anything, to hear. She went back upstairs and took three Nytol pills, enough to knock her out imagelessly for eight hours.

The yellow cymbal-clash of sound was the front door. Her father had returned home, it was Sunday evening and the house was flooded with greasy blackness, with soundless engine-oil shadows. Her mind flipped over dates and memories like a paper aeroplane trying to stay atop the wind: Friday school, Saturday clothes, today. What was today? Underneath all that, even in the unconscious seamless sleep, flowed a dense matted river of melancholy, a dead-bodies-and-trash canal of misery, a plastic paddling-pool of self-pity. Get up, she said to herself. Get up and get ready. Dinner with Juliane.

– 'Pale?'

Her father stood over her bed.

– 'Are you OK?'

She tried to talk through the thick bandage of drowsiness.

– 'I took some sleeping pills.'

He held her hand.

– 'You shouldn't take pills. You need a shower.'

– 'Mmm. I'll have one. Soon. I have to go out.'

– 'I know. Juliane called to see if you were still going out to meet him.'

– 'You spoke to him?'

– 'For a while. Don't you dare come back late –'

– 'When did he call?'

– 'About fifteen minutes ago. Didn't you hear it?'

She turned her head, looked at the wall in front of her face.

– 'I thought you just got in.'

He shook his head.

– 'About an hour ago.'

– 'I feel sick.'

She lurched up.

– 'My head hurts.'

She started crying; her father put his arm around her.

– 'Don't worry. I know you feel bad. I'll run you a bath.'

She wrapped her arms around him and smelled cigarettes, not his own brand, a different aftershave, his car, sweat, unfamiliar shampoo. She felt a punchbag-thud of curiosity and was going to ask about his conference, but her head was a lumbering bear of pain, her eyeballs two heavy spheres filled with iron filings in a skull insulated with brown paper and bubble-wrap. Her tongue felt enormous and furry, her eyelashes were crusted with yellow, her nose gummed up.

She lay back in the bath, aromatherapy oil and bubbles gelling together to form a cellophane layer on the surface, kiwi fruit conditioner in her hair, avocado mask on her face, apple body-wash down her limbs; orchid milk cleanser, dewberry moisturiser, some splashes of musk perfume. Her father shouted up from the living-room:

173

– I love it when you take a bath. The whole house smells like an exotic greengrocer's.'
– 'Do you want me?'
– 'Come down for a second before you get ready, if you want.'

She went down to see him, and for half an hour she let the thoughts be blitzed out of her head as they lay on the couch, pleasure stacked on to pleasure in explosions of violence, bruising and biting, purrs, gasps, sighs, all the variations of non-words, of expressive non-expressions, rough changes of position, heat, whose ardour swiped away past and future and that little pitch of her mind was blanker than endless miles of undisturbed shore. She saw the ridges of his chest, the jut of ribs and hipbones, the sweat-silvered hair and rigid arm-lean above her.

Two hours later, Juliane was looking at her over his board of sushi, while she toyed with her sashimi. He said:
– 'You don't like it?'

She did like it, she liked the purity of flavour, the soft delicacy of the flesh, she liked the colours – peacock-feather blue, petal-pink, jade green, fuchsia-purple, eggshell-yellow; she even liked the restaurant, with its smooth benches and tables set out in the soft-lit wood rooms like stacks of shortbread on a pine sideboard. She looked out and saw bicycle couriers feeble in the white-grey December night, couples cuddling together, hatchet-faced people in suits and sensible oatmeal-coloured overcoats.

She didn't like Juliane, who in under an hour had quoted to her from both *Measure for Measure* and *The Whitsun Weddings*, incorrectly, and made imperfect references to Mao's China, Clinton and the UN, Malcolm X and sodium's relationship with water. He talked about films, about songs they'd both heard on the radio, about the literary classics; he asked her views: What do you think – ... What's your favour- ite – ... If you were ... What would you – ... how would you go about – ... Under what circumstances might you ... He was funny, they got on, she didn't like him.

She only began to enjoy herself when, after the meal, they sat in their cab and he pointed to some pedestrian they passed, letting the back of his hand brush the side of her breast. The driver was watching them through the rear-view mirror, one corned-beef hand on the wheel, his puffed grey eyes half-hidden behind tinted beige glasses, his uneven potato-chin peeking from behind the grey anorak. She put her hand around the composer's wrist, her thumb and fingers not meeting, and held his arm against the seat. The driver coughed, thousands of par- ticles of spit ping-ponging in the back of his throat, black- bodied in the nicotine palace of his lungs. Juliane felt her chest pressing into his, her small strength and tight back, the bumps of vertebrae beneath the fluffy burnt-leaves colour of her jumper, her velvet knee digging into his thigh. He easily pushed her back against the vinyl, which smelled of white spirit and dog and kebab, cupped her face in his hands and said:
– 'Slow down.'
– 'Sorry.'
The sharp point of his tongue probed her gums. They looked at each other, onyx irises against opal, and that old unname- able heartscan-blip of understanding sparked for a second, before being lost in the Ford Escort tyre-shriek of an ignored red light. She clamped her front teeth around his lower lip, her hands in his hair. He repeated:

– 'Things hurt. I know that. Make a decision.'

The driver rolled down the window, snorted and spat, a bullet of grey slime hurtling audibly through the Christmas chill on to the kerb. As a shiny buttercup-yellow car with thudding techno on its sound system drew up next to the cab at a set of lights, he arranged his peeling sausage-in-batter fingers offensively, and rumbled something about young people these days. Another rip-snort, and this time the greeny pellet hit the hub-cap of the banana-coloured disco car.

In bed that night Pale wondered what Juliane had been talking about, and was unable to peg her memories down, catch on to the flapping sheet of meaning and stake it out on a patch of absolute truth. Three orders' worth of sake took her out on its gentle crescent-shaped canoe, barely cracking the water, and rocked her to sleep.

Will had always sung in the shower, hummed to himself in the bath, whistled a few tunes while making tea. When he screwed, sometimes he heard entire symphonies, sometimes scores of famous films, sometimes jingles from the radio. Occasionally, the glib lyrics of pop songs would pelt out of his mouth when he least wanted them to. He hadn't expected to find himself talking to the empty air, though. But there it was. He would wake up and a stream of chatter would spill out from his lips, a community of voices, a machine-gun-fire of jokes, of nonsensical phrases; he talked to the ceiling, he talked to his own reflection, he talked to the kettle and the bookshelves, his computer. Each object had a different manner of address, a different tone; he'd spit out vengeful couplets and rhyming slang and sombre soliloquies in impeccable iambic pentameter. Sometimes it was a monologue, at other times a chorus, more often than not the half-enunciated bumbles and squeaks of a baby, occasionally the cracked-stone vowels of an old man. When he got the cufflinks, he burst into tears.

Work was holding his neck and forcing him down under the surface. Work was strapping him to a table and sending a laser-saw up between his legs. Work had his shoulders viced in a rugby scrum of timetabling and politics; it had him in a ballroom dance of ferocious complexity. Work had him in a headlock. Juliane tapped him on the shoulder one afternoon.
– 'How's it all going?'
– 'Oh, fine.'

He loved the media, generously and exultantly; he loved the city and how easy it was to get hold of smack and coke and whiz, those narcotic single-syllable words whose slang sounded so brilliantly youthfully fierce: a request to the right person, the person low enough to go looking, sniffing around for it, and these days it came complete with dinky DHL stamp and an Enjoy Your Parcel Sir, or was handed over by a plague-faced youth in a Parcelforce uniform, or wearing a Blue Arrow cap. Something adolescent in him loved the snorting and squirting, the streaming eyes and liquifying sinuses, the gilded blood-rush, the eyeball-straining dot-pupiled concentration, the nocturnal energy and mercury-veined calm, the leopard-prowl endurance. Wired, caned, wasted, plastered, stoned, steaming, buzzing, coming up, those dirty-sounding words; the furtive colloquialism of pharmaceutical privilege inflated and ballooned in his head. Of course, he'd done it all before, buoyantly lifted up on white-crested waves of – what had he called it all then? – angel dust, snow; before the early-thirties vegetarianism, the just-a-mineral-water absten-tion, the experiments with brown rice. Ginseng's the only drug you need.

There was nothing wrong with it. For the time that he was working, his brain was a piston-pump of lucidity, a mechan-ized relay race of creative activity. Ideas flipped and arced, triple-jointed, across his frontal lobe; the diplomat in him trapezed and tightrope-walked, stoically stern; he delegated, he listened, he debated, he directed. On the farthest curve of his fish-eyed vision lurked Juliane, with his scythe-edge jaw and cupid's-bow brow, displaying his amphibian scale of win-ter colours, a sartorially elegant praying mantis hopping and darting in a puff of manuscript paper. He became just another employee, a colleague.

On the Wednesday a truck with mashing jaws came along the street, boss-eyed and yellow-scaled in the matt winter brownness, and chewed up the squat red box with its folds of strawberry-coloured tissue, and two silver hearts clinked against each other before they were minced and mulched and masticated and came out looking like two lost fillings, scrunched-up sweetpaper, bent coins, tinkling about next to the banana-skins, the milk cartons, the cereal boxes, the old magazines and mouldy bread and used condoms and useless pens and gobbed-into tissues.

On the Thursday Will went up to Krishan, his assistant. There was always a current of racial unease between them, an askance over-awareness of each other's skin tone. It would have been better if one was wholly clever, the other wholly attractive; one tall and slender, the other stocky and muscle-packed. Krishan was talking to one of the actresses, his lion-mane of golden wave flipping between narrow fingers as he looked down at her, the spiciness of Havana For Men enfolding them both. Will waited for his assistant's attention, then:

– 'Krish?'

– 'Yeah?'

Private school, moderate middle-classness, Oxford or Cambridge – same difference – it was all there in one laconic word.

Will said:

– 'Can you take over for the afternoon? I need a break. I feel like I'm going to collapse.'

– 'Stop pretending to be a junkie then.'

The startling pale grey eyes looked at him, Botticelli-lashed; he smirked. The razor-strap body readjusted itself in the Versace suit, the hair-thin gold necklace flashed discreetly, that torso was all angles under his shirt. His mind full of pictures of child prostitutes and Calcutta slums, shitting into holes, Bollywood, packs and herds of cockroaches, Will said:

– 'Why don't you stop fucking the leading lady, then?'

– 'Because if anything it's helping my work. It's good PR. Things might be going well now but you're on a cliff-edge and you'll burn out or lose it or crack up at some point.'

A pause.

– 'I'm telling you this as a friend.'

A cab to Oxford Street, past the hats and coats and harassed faces of Christmas shoppers, an army of mothers, a tidal wave of anxious boyfriends. He was thinking of the two dancing sparks of the cufflinks, their streaky silver-white calibre and the flush of . . . the sense that he was wanted, that he was

thought of, the ego-swell of knowing he had captivated someone. He bought a suit in sable brown, in a fabric that felt like
silk and moved more softly than cream spiralling into coffee,
a blue V-necked jumper that fitted closely along his sides,
black leather gloves whose sheen reminded him of Pale's hair.
He posed and rucked up his collar and looked world-weary
and turbulent in Caffe Nero and Mondo and Bar Italia and
Patisserie Valerie, even though he was invariably the oldest
person there. There was artificial happiness flowing through
his veins, and artificial confusion clouding his sight, and
occasionally pelting showers of artificial irritation; optimism
coated the inside of his nose, energy was under his gums,
permissiveness was lining his throat. He opened his wallet and
looked at the kaleidoscope of plastic, the gallery of mono-
grams and logos: AmEx, Visa, Mastercard, Access, a glut of
individual store cards. Money was evaporating off him; every
breath that floated away white-sailed in the air was worth fifty
quid, every cough a grand. Every puke every night dredged up
glittering crystals, wafts of powder, tadpoles of blood, snakes
of black slime.

Work had him in an expert tackle, down on the ground
with everything blurring around him. Work was shovelling
dirt into his open mouth, glueing his eyelids shut, sewing his
fingers together. Work was holding him to ransom, silver pis-
tol to the temple. Work was somewhere face-to-face with his
naked groin, angling a razor thoughtfully with salsa playing
in the background.

And on Friday, party time, he had his first one-night stand
in four months. Found her standing by the bar, one of the
straps of her black dress slipping down a plumpish shoulder,

koala-eyes slightly milky in the crush; she worked in wardrobe, or something; she had a body shaped like a double-bass, and cackled like a chimp when she came.

ten

December

*The last few hours of my stay. Ian has gone out walking alone –
his new hobby. I'm sitting here on the sofa reading magazines
and books and doodling and writing in my diary. I wonder what
he thinks when he's out there; he doesn't seem the type to glance
about and think and exclaim to himself: Why, the circularity of
those dustbin-lids, the grainy haphazardness of these urban
pathways, the humbling wreckage of that windowless car, the
irregular scrawl of that graffiti! He's not an observer, a
charismatic spectator, a lover of the outside world. He doesn't
marvel at the grandeur of nature, the stateliness of the passing
seasons, he doesn't pause to consider the grinding machine of
the city. He's like a worm curling away from an advancing shoe-
edge; it's only comfort and discomfort, with him.*

So, the job with the composer is over. One letter, a telephone exchange, a final pay-packet, and now Ian's rage has spread around and floodgated out. The whole house swims and rumbles with his rage, with his claustrophobia, and I hide myself away, ten times more evil than he is, probably, but I'm a woman, so I unravel my lunacy on the pages of this book. The metaphors for Ian are cheap and ancient: the subdued force of a caged animal who can remember its old wildness, the spiritual fanaticism of someone on death row, an orphan butting its head against the wall, trapped inside its own world. He's started walking. Where d'you go? I ask him. Just around, he says. Around the block, around the town, around the tubeline, or what? I ask him. He doesn't seem to know; inside his brain is a personalized map of places seen, routes marked out, a contour-scan of streets and corners that fascinate him and others he feels it's fine to ignore. He's young, he's barely lived, and he's already started the walking, the treading-out of ideas, the patting-down of mental action.

The last few pages of this diary smell of this house, of the soaps and liquids in my brother's bathroom. Sometimes it pleases me to sit at night and read back through the last year or half-year, and trace the line of woe – such a brilliant word, the woe of Louisa Gradgrind and Lucy Snowe, that nineteenth-century welling of despair – through to the previous evening. Because I know it never changes, as a bird-call doesn't alter through the seasons though it may go from coast to coast.

Of course it's happened. The day of the split with Juliane I could feel his tension morse-coding itself from Hertfordshire, electric-

wiring me to him; I could practically feel the jiggle of the
Edgware bus under my feet, the clack of the Northern Line train,
the crush of King's Cross; I could smell the urine-air of Holloway
Road station, Arsenal station, Turnpike Lane station, the
coldness of the streets outside. I took a shower and went into the
kitchen to wait, looking at a neighbour's cat stepping among the
slush-clumps in the back garden and wondering whether this was
one of the shaggers, the ear-splitting screamers who screw every
night beneath the window and keep me awake. The slam of the
front door, then the three creaks of his steps as he came over to
the kitchen where I was tactfully stirring or tasting something
from the pan on the hob. Soup, broth, stew – something
comfortable and matronly, to warm the base of the stomach.

I'm still not clear about the politics of it all: was he sacked, did
he quit, was it amicable? I think it was a whim. I think it was
one of those jobs you lose by a shrug of the shoulders, a post
cancelled by a flick of the wrist, prospects clouded by one
moment's anger, a fatally dramatic exit, a blast of words. When I
asked him about it, he couldn't meet my eyes. He'll exist on his
savings, he says; he's been putting about half away. His savings
account must be like a cavern of curled notes, grimy coins, a sty
of piggy-banks, a heavy gold testament to a cautious nature.
And, the classic male answer, something will come along.

Women know all about this. Some things don't come along.
There is never anyone waiting with a vision of you as their ideal.
Women know that what they fulfil is never the whole, they never
vindicate others' dreams in their totality. Women know that they
are the seconds, the settled-for, the just-acceptable. Women learn

to take whatever is offered, because they suspect – actually, they know – that the gold disc of sunny success glimpsed from beyond the rocky precipices of the present is probably just the reflection of some cheap nylon businessman's fake Rolex.

But you can't say anything, because men like Ian will never understand their own error. You just nod in that way, the way that makes them think how right they are, and say: Oh, yes. I'm sure something'll come along, in time. You have to watch your tone of voice: too terse, too sarcastic, and a little mite of reality, of actually understanding, might chip and munch its way suddenly into the great wooden gallery of their self-confidence.

So I'm there in the too-tight life jacket of his hug. Funny what things'll run through your mind in situations like that – my first consideration was for the soup I'd been making, the closeness of my palm to the hot side of the pan. Then my face was pressed flat into his chest, and I thought: There's no air in here, I'll suffocate. I think he knew it, or else he was stronger than he realized, because when I began to twist away, just to breathe in, not to get away from him, he held on more tightly.

By the time we were both without shirts, caught in that rush of physical impulse, the desperation to touch, those staccato breaths and suction-pump kisses which are always shameful and embarrassing when you think about them later, I knew I could have been anyone. He just wanted a body. It prompted something in me, a wake-up call, an alarm-scream of awareness. I was reconnected with that endless high voltage of violence I'd identified in John, and let myself be taken in by. You can't say

*no to power like that, you can't negate something so primal. I
won't call it rape, because I understand, now – and almost
sympathize – with what it is in them that wants to hurt us. I
won't forget the redness of his chest, the tension of thigh and
stomach, that warped expression on his face. His eyes locked on
to mine halfway through and the spatial black of his pupils, the
threads of vein and tiny creases of muscle and lid around them
expressed hate in its purest form, clear and elegant and full of
bitterness. We screwed and screwed, strenuously then gleefully
and then exhaustedly. There are marks all over me.*

Christmas came down and suffocated London like a trunkful
of grey bedsheets, heavy, loft-dusty and smelling of age.
Oxford Street was a taupe walkway of iron shutters and
switched-off shoplights, of displayed clothes which already
looked dated. In the gutters and puddles basked old tube
tickets, fast-food greasepaper, lost gloves, abandoned maps,
drinks cans; Charing Cross Road was a grey fuzz of escaping
traffic, Tottenham Court Road a pencil-smudge of cement.
Soho Square was a locked railinged patch of dead plants and
black grass through which isolated pigeons picked and pocked
dismally. In between the cobbles of Covent Garden were
unidentifiable bits of mess: torn-up paper, chewing-gum, a
smattering of copper coins, the tired pinkish disc of dropped
tomato from a sandwich. Piccadilly Circus was a ghostland
of big business and big entertainment, of gloss and glass and
ads and cinema-signs, the dry bleak width echoing with its
bareness. The people out in the middle of London at Christmas
were the ones with no families or friends, though not homeless,
not vagrants, the unthought-of band who stuck themselves

beneath the smallest ledge of the employment scale, occupied
the trickiest nook of immigration law: tan-anoraked, scarves
bobbling and furring like mangy cats, blue-jeaned with
wrinkled trainers, woolly-gloved hands in zip-pockets, dreads
and long curls of hair tucked into collars or underneath black
wool fishermen's caps, sometimes a pink flash of nearly-shaven
skull.

People were embedded in the red heat of their front rooms,
wedged against the loaded debris of extendable dining tables,
comatose in their armchairs. Christmas was a chorus of fight-
ing family voices, of adolescent whines and female anger and
male trappedness, of pensioner irritation and grandparent
wheedling; Christmas flipped back the covers on the oldest
feuds, the loudest unspoken grudges, the petty hatreds that
had festered over the year; everyone sat in that one room
sharing turkey breath and mince belches, tarry pudding snores
and gravy coughs.

Even those who didn't celebrate, whose homes remained
unmarked by silver-paper angels and reflective baubles and the
tack of fake trees, were locked indoors for those five distended
watery afternoons of burning familial–religious fervour. By
Boxing Day Ian was striding sullenly around and around the
block, kicking cardboard boxes and empty plastic litre-bottles
out of the way, nudging broken prams and shopping trolleys
aside, sneering with recognition at all the other men out walking, champing out their frustration on the uneven paving
stones, the crumbling kerbs, the faded zebra crossings of Turnpike Lane. He climbed over the low railings of the children's
park and sat on the car-tyre swings, the scaffolding-planks of
climbing-frame, the dry blue tongue of the slide, the wooden

slats of the roundabout. A man in a baby-blue velour tracksuit jogged by him; two teenaged boys in football shirts and over-sized trainers skittered, ignoring the cold; a woman with a waist-length plait of burnt-siena hair walked slowly with her young daughter, glancing at him.

Up in Ruislip.
– 'Dad –'
– 'I'm going to the office. Work to do.'
– 'Isn't it shut? It is Christmas, in case you hadn't noticed.'
– 'My office, my key. I can go in there any time I want. Is there food in?'
– 'Yeah, of course –'
– 'See you, then. I'll be back late. If there're any calls for me –'
– 'I'll give them the office number.'

So Pale was left in the tawny squashy velvet pocket of the sitting-room, the chunky sofa and armchairs and fat cushions and rug dusty in the day's light, the impassive plane of the dining table stacked with her GCSE Revision Guide, her tower of notes and textbooks and tin of biros, her pencil sharpener and eraser and Pritt Stick and Tipp-Ex and geometry set in a little cluster, all unused as yet. The kitchen work-top was crunchy with sugar, with puddles and globules of fat, melting in slow drips of syrup and sauce and seasoning, crinkling shinily in their plastic wrappers, their moulded display-trays, their selection-boxes and value packs, tied up with Buy One Get One Free sellotape.

*

– 'Hello?'
– 'Juliane, it's Pale.'
– 'Oh, hi.'
– 'Were you busy?'
– 'Sort of.'
– 'Can't you speak?'
– 'Not really. Sorry.'
– 'Are you entertaining?'
– 'Composing. The deadline is everything.'

The one red eye at the top of the Lodge was crusted over with ice; now pink, it cast its light inside, a rabbity albino wash on the upstairs landing. The bedroom, aggressively unfurnished apart from the determined black square of bed, evoked a waltz of vodka and old aftershave and cigarettes, and the sweet/sour/fresh/rank Highland Fling of sweat; it smelled of unwashed clothes and reused underwear, yellow unbrushed teeth, unshaven flesh. Downstairs, Juliane put the phone down on Pale – whose voice triggered an inconvenient spillage of sexual recollection – and went back into the studio at the back of the house, slamming the door.

There were bite marks on his neck, nail-crescents on his shoulders, a triple speed-stripe of scratches on his back, two lavender bruise-clouds on his sides. His professional thoughts were being accordioned aside by the remembered images of a small-fingered fist tangled in his hair, the double-curved underside of a vanilla-white chest, the indentation of waist and incline of hips. Ten days, nearly ten screws; but he had to work, so he'd decided to remove her like a surgeon extracts offending slivers of metal from bone, to fish her out and flick her into the distance, trample and then sweep her away into the coal-scuttle of the past, the cobweb-curtained cellar of historic events.

The phone rang again, the separate line – with its separate number – in the studio.

– 'Juliane?'

– 'Will. I was expecting your call. Not celebrating Christmas, I take it?'

– 'Tell me about it. Tell me how the music's going.'

– 'Well. It's going well. Are you OK?'

– 'You'll be around for the rest of the filming? The filming goes on –'

– 'Three days out of five, and I want a tape as soon as you can get hold of one. Doesn't matter if it's not the final edit.'

– 'It'll be there. Don't worry. I never seem to stop talking to people about things.'

– 'I know. This is good, isn't it?'

– 'Yeah. It's good. We can do this. It's happening.'

– 'No diversions?'

– 'None whatsoever, except the puking. You?'

– 'When is there ever?'

The New Year hunched up and squatted greasily behind the flashy tart of Christmas week, pallid-complexioned and protectively wrapped in rough layers of grey fog, a sodden jerkin of sleety snow and flapping rainy trousers. London woke out of its anaesthesia, rolling bulbous-veined and wrinkle-cheeked back into action. For the first three weeks of January, the city was vague and slit-eyed, blinking blindly in the harsh dawn of re-started time, pinkly bald like a newborn puppy.

Now Juliane was on his own again the ideas had come with more speed, with the crash of a broken dam, a roaring echo-chamber of re-realized inspiration pickaxing down through all the levels of his brain. It was left for him to sit and sift through the cramped junk-loaded boudoir of reinvigorated talent, to sort and organize and plan. The writing and performance were the easiest parts. He'd always said it: good art was an administrative job.

Dear Ian,

I thought you might appreciate a list of what I saw when I got back home: all the mail I'd received torn into pieces beside the mat; John's muddy winter-jacket on the un-hoovered floor with the broken coathook lying next to it, still attached to a chunk of plaster; a pile of empty carrier bags from the local supermarket; folds of old newspapers; a full bin bag that hadn't been taken out.

The kitchen was the best: black-crusted bowls, scummy dinner plates, saucers each with an oval of dried coffee, a thin smile of spilt tea; an assembly of tumblers, each half-full of flat coke or green milk; a packet of damp furry bread, foetid cheese, plastic containers for houmus and guacamole and taramasalata, one with a fly stuck in it; an open tub of margarine sprinkled with toast-crumbs; an army of knives and forks coated with the residue of peas and white chips, baked beans; a skittle-run of empty beer and wine bottles. So what did I do? I started cleaning, of course. Ooh, these men, I could hear my superego tutting, arms crossed, Need a woman around to liven the place up. Make it home. Down on my knees, skirt tucked up into my knickers, sleeves rolled up, cleaning away.

No tree, no fairy-lights in the window, no presents hidden in the corner, no Welcome Back! sign, no cards, no Mr Kipling's mince pies in the fridge, no mightily tanned poultry on an oven tray. He was upstairs, in a stupor, in that grey flannel tracksuit, the snot-coloured cardigan, those towelling sports-socks with the snazzy blue stripe across the top, little gold Argos pendant sliding off his neck and wedging into the red space of his ear. He was snoring again.

It's cold here. No – it's cold everywhere but it's freezing here. It's Arctic, it's cold enough to freeze your eyebrows into place, chisel your toes off into little blue nuggets rolling about inside your shoes, desensitize your mouth so much you don't know if you're smiling or not, though you probably aren't. From the window at the front of the house I can see into the front room of the house opposite, where a man in a television-fuzz jumper – Mr Collins or Jones or Matthews or Baker, we met him once – is sitting writing letters and his woman, faded in a faded dress, drinks from a teacup. This place is so depressing people don't even stick around to mess it up. There are no children's playthings in the gardens, no blast of teenagers' stereos, no flash cars, nobody who lives here ever invites their relatives down for a visit. The neighbourhood cats are too depressed to fuck. They're probably busy poring over train timetables and travel brochures planning their next getaway.

There's clothes need washing. That's the first thing he said to me, when he came round. He knows how to speak – John puts on that pedantic Fulham Council vowel-snivel every morning, along with his shiny-bottomed suit, his suede elbow-patched jacket. But at home he lapses, he's lazy. We're married: there need be no secrets; there's no place to hide, in the linguistics of marital life. So he says, There's clothes need washing, There's dirty cups in that there sink and, pointing, That's the rubbish needs taking out. And his questions are, Is it taken out, the rubbish? Are they cleaned, the pots? And when it's relationship-stuff, girl-stuff, his whole sentence construction goes and he becomes an orang-utan of single-word ejaculations and emphatic statement: You love me. You live here. I married you. It is impossible to hold a conversation with someone like John.

And that was that, Ian. Can you imagine? Two hours after returning home, I was hunched over the sink with a wooden brush trying to get a two-month-old stripe of dirt off one of his shirt-collars. He'd love it if we lived in the type of house where all the food was made in one giant beaten tin pan, and I ironed our things with the kind of instrument that you have to heat up over the fire and test with a dampened forefinger. But there you go. It was comfortable, it was familiar, scratching that brush along the collar, hands reddening, neck beginning to hurt.

It took me hours to get the kitchen back in order, and then he took me to bed. Actually, no. He didn't grasp me by the hand and lead me up a rose-crammed lane to a warm dusky love-bower. Of course not. He didn't undress me layer by layer and – what? – plant a lily-garden of kisses on my skin. But then neither did you. I cleaned the kitchen, then I cleaned the bedroom, then he came in and closed the door behind him and stood against it. So, once more, I had no choice.

I've started walking too, and I think I understand you all the better for it. Under my coat I wear two vests, two pairs of tights, tracksuit bottoms rather than jeans, thick socks, my old trainers, sweatshirt and jumper. I wrap a scarf around my head 'til only the eyes show; I like the difference in my appearance. It makes me into even more of a nobody – I look like every ignored fat girl in every class. I go round the block and up to the High Street, then I walk further on; I measure out my walks by bus-routes in case I get tired. It feels good to know that I can walk far, if ever I have to. I always thought, in the last weeks, that you went out walking to sort out your thoughts, as if a five-hundred-yard stroll meant you came back with them all index-carded and alphabetical, stacked according to size, marker-penned and proofread, displayed in a flow-chart of priorities and projected on to the inside of your skull. But I think I understand. You know when you're making a bed, new sheets, new pillow-covers, new everything? You flip your arms up high, slide your hands far apart, and the sheet unfurls against the bright window like every fabric-softener commercial you've ever seen. That clean liquid breaking-open movement is how your thoughts go, when you're walking. When I come back from a walk I can never remember what I've been thinking about.

But I have made a decision. My visit to you was the experiment, and here is my answer. Here is what I inferred, deduced. I have begun looking at men, at boys, and young male children. All the gender is one, to me. I've seen them gather on street corners and howl at the moon, cans of cider in hand; I've seen them sweetly squeeze the slim behinds of their girlfriends; I've seen them step out of restaurants and hand their mistresses into cabs with the chivalry of Lancelot; I've seen them on their own in women's clothes shops, worriedly plucking at dresses and tops and flimsier items, and I've seen their lips moving in that baffled mantra of possible sizes; I've seen them out on the pitch, the field, the court, lunging together, barking complaints and commands at each other, rollicking in the mud like dogs. I am in awe of their energy, the connectivity of the masculine psyche.

Sometimes I don't know what to think. There are sweet ones: the slightly fatter, the gangly, the shorter-than-average, the studenty ones with good skin and bright clothes weighed down with labels, the youngish fathers with their children bobbing four feet in front of them in red dungarees and blue caps, holding – probably – those plastic windmill-things that kids seem to love. I sit on benches and watch them move past me.

But generally I think each man is linked by his anger to the next, that each is one more hard little knot in a net of enraged strength; this kind of rage is a letterbomb, ticking unconsciously, discreetly, before destroying everything in its vicinity. In this net, this mesh, this tapestry of anger are all variations of irritation and all attendant shades of fear, there is every type of loneliness and every sub-particle of hopelessness. While with women it might convert itself into an eternal listlessness, a watching-old-films bitterness, weeping, or it might, more likely, simply sink down slowly and mould itself to the deepest recesses of her identity, clenching there for the rest of her life, men will strut their anger, fan it out like a peacock's tail, beat out the insistent rhythm of their Why Not Me? and What Happened? and Who Forgot Me? It is always, always the same. Men are continually amazed by the misery in their own lives.

Nearly the last paragraph. Don't worry. You don't have to shuffle my letter, flick the pages over impatiently to search for the coy scribble of my sign-off. I'm staying. Here I am. We married. Is it married we are? Fulham is my home and, well, there is nowhere else to go. I know nobody, I have no job, no qualifications, except the borstal-toil of marriage. Find someone, get away. Those tiny phrases of escape – break free, cut loose, follow your dreams, flee – mean nothing. Every woman everywhere is being beaten, is being raped, is cleaning some shit-strewn bathroom, wiping neck-grease and crotch-scum off underclothes, is being used somehow. Every woman everywhere is dreaming of escape, and there is nowhere we can go.

So I stay. It is, after all, my house. Those are my clothes in that wardrobe, that is my work which keeps the dishes in their sparkling stack on the shelves. I know no other men, except you, and you know that we could never be together. All that rage, yours and mine. We'd burn the street down!

Think of me, in that cold house of yours.

Sophie.

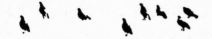

eleven

All of London is bent quivering and bare-backsided in front of the sun's mallet-smack of heat. June has been a stampede of too-sultry days: everywhere are rippling wet foreheads, mushy lips coated with bobbles of perspiration, pockets of fluid dripping down torsoes inside shirts, slick palms, feet sliding inside their shoes. The streets are too hot to walk on, the mirror-glare of shop windows, the screaming brightness of cars, the roads are turning into swamps of tar, the sticky breath of everyone else. Even in the shade the creeping fingers of heat sidle inside waistbands, feel along pockets, poke about inside collars, jab into eyeballs. The cool reading-a-book-outdoors flush of spring has been flattened out under the stiletto-grind of the summer months.

But inside the school it's like a water-cooler, an icebox, a

Thermos of goosebumps and sudden shivers and blue finger-tips and thudding headaches, of extra jumpers and more coffee and dissipating energy. Ms Steel churns on her casters around the corridors, checking and monitoring and administering fear, handing it out, giving it away for free, some for everyone. Lovejoy warbles and trills – one day her glasses are lilac-tinted, another day they're a jaunty saffron yellow; her chiffon scarves show pictures of cherubs, of hieroglyphics, of rose-petals and geometric Arabic patterns, as she hounds the bunkers and skivers.

Inside the main hall, the one used for assemblies and prize-givings, concerts and gymnastics displays, are ranks and col-umns and rows of desks, each a little creaky, a little reluctant to be unfolded and staked out there, beached on the wooden floor still with its old netball-court markings in white paint. And behind each desk is a static riot of plastic chair, mar-ginally too low, a fraction too wide to fit under the table, one leg a smidgen short. The hall smells of feet, old sandwiches, hymn-books, dust, wood-varnish; one of the dozen long tube-lights blinks confusedly, clicks and winks and shudders. The air, normally a mass of sunlit fluff winding dreamily up to meet the asbestos, is rigid with concentration, with tension. Something slack in that hall throughout the year – the sleepy-brained prayers at nine o'clock every day, the slack-bottomed first-years in leotards on Wednesday afternoons, the memory of tiny-skirted girls from the 1960s flipping a netball between them, the boredom of parents at another evening of sawing cellos and Requiem – has now been pulled tight. Every face over every desk has in its smooth oval jaw, its unmarked plane of forehead and serene tilt of eyelid the iron bolts of stamina, the girders of memory, the rafters and ropes and pulleys of active knowledge. Every tendon in that wrist strikes a tabla-ripple of pain with each scratch of the pen, the agonized punctuating and lining of letters, the streaks of comma and dot-slash of semi-colon.

The long black spine of the minute-hand is flexing resolutely around the clock-surface; a dozen faces gaze at it, although their pens don't stop. In their eyes is fear, the pure immediate basic fear of animals caught in headlights, of gun-barrel threats, of cars and people glimpsed minute from narrow high bridges. Teachers patrol the aisles between the desks remembering their own first exams, looking at that glut of raw youth hemmed into the hall. Not one face is scarred with acne, yet, not one stomach bisected with a Caesarean scar, no limbs lost; these kids have not known accidents or death, have not yet understood distance or travel. They'll learn, think the adults vengefully; their time will come.

Pale is fucking up. She sits, her thighs stuck to her plastic seat, her back an electric scratch-board of diagonal itches beneath the polyester jumper, and knows that every word she is writing is bullshit, that her ideas signify nothing and her conclusions are simply exuberantly-worded lies. Identify the different types of moral ambivalence in *Measure for Measure*. What is Larkin's view of love? Analyse Browning's 'My Last Duchess' with reference to the poetic viewpoint, structure and imagery. She knows these questions, has gone over them before, has mental images of them – millions of crazily slanted words crossed with teachers' red marker-pen. When did she do those essays? Last winter, last autumn? She writes on, with her sloppy quotes and convoluted sentences, her misplaced pronouns and cautiously introduced colons, her wild lyricism and giant empty statements. The minute-hand rolls.

She's done this for every exam, for every subject. There is still a week left to go. She knew the stuff once, she knew about different layers of soil and the Great Exhibition and Angelo's vulnerability and the heat-conducting powers of copper. Her intellect used to be a science-fiction laser-zap of concentrated thought, a predatory invader-ship of inquisitive questions; she was one of those who had that telepathic speed of comprehension, the kind that translates only partially on paper. None the less, she'd known about isosceles triangles, about density, mass and volume, about the past participle and the imperfect tense. But her head's now a flat concrete canal-bank past which no dark barge laden with facts flows. Instead, her thoughts snag on incidental spikes, wedge into unseen cracks, are entangled in suddenly-grabbing vines. And she's writing bullshit – flagrant, effusive, colossal reams of prime bullshit are oozing out of her fibre-tip on to the sixth sheet of lined paper.

Ten days, now, ten days she's been pregnant. Or rather, she found out ten days ago. The stomach-rumble, the abdomen-squeak, the liver-burble, the bowel-crunch: it isn't hunger. The backache, a creak of pain behind the shoulder-blades, a bout of midnight nausea, the unexpected tiredness: those are the signs, the phantom almost-symptoms telling you to check. So there's a torn-apart test in the bottom drawer of the chest at home, with its frantically-unfolded instruction leaflet, and the rest has been thrown away, after the two little dots changed colour, and she found out, no, her thoughts were confirmed.

So she knows only this, that there's a translucent worm of

fragile skin inside her, a slime-pellet of growing flesh. She imagines a feeble tadpole with human eyes, a bulbous-headed slug with a giant purple heart, a grass-snake with human hands, a wet ball of unmoulded clay for a brain, a flaky dry bric-à-brac heap of genes. Just add water. She wonders if it grows a limb at a time, building up like a plasticine model; she wonders if she'll be able to feel it jolting as she runs, like a test dummy in a speeding car, anchored with its umbilical seatbelt.

More than that, she can't consider. She knows she wants to get rid of it, and with every cough, every shit she takes, every set of stairs she bounds down to catch up with her friend Holly, momentarily forgetting, she hopes its pin-head brain has folded in a tiny meteor-burst of declension, cracked under the pressure, she hopes its noodle-limbs and brush-stroke digits jam together like kneaded dough when she sleeps on her stomach at night, she wants to force a fist up herself and yank it all out, stuff the jellied mess into the waste disposal system and grind the load into a mousse of DNA.

The long hand makes its final revolution. Teachers march down the columns of desks, collecting up papers. Outside, Pale can see the yellow wellington-boot of sunshine pounding on the prep school's playground. She peers back and across at Holly, who raises her eyebrows in an exhausted sympathetic look. They go together to collect bags but separate in the furnace of the school's front lawn. Pale, with the iodine-stain of failure blotting her mind, with the strawberry-jam blob of child inside her, numbly watches her friend get on to the bus – a wave, a jokey face – before making her way to the tube station. Her hair irritates her, smacking into her eyes then lying smooth as flame over her neck, getting caught in the arm-squeeze as she holds on to the rucksack. She's tied the jumper around her waist, so now her pelvis is a rocking cradle of man-made discomfort, prickly and intense, but she's too tired to carry it. Summer is draining things out of her. She has to go home; Daddy is waiting.

Summer is easy with air-conditioning, as Ian knows. He sits behind his desk, just back from a long lunch, and his shirt-sleeved forearms lie like bolsters on the black steel. The furniture is dated but he feels its aggression suits him; he likes to look about the open-plan emporium of steel and chrome, the squeaking pyramids of leather and glass, the arcade of clicking knick-knacks and narrow-framed Rothko prints. But he likes the modern world too, he likes the turning-on, the light-flick of electric convenience, the switch-command of power; he likes the voice which greets him whenever he picks up the phone, his computer-kinship with the rest of the city, maybe possibly the world, if he can take on his own ambition and win.

Every afternoon at three-thirty the new girl comes up to his desk and pours coffee for him. It helps him get sober again for late work. He watches her approach, that small self-conscious stride in fashionable mail-order clothes, her authentic high-street style. Her eyes meet the shadows of his; she can't tell if he is watching her, if she should put some curl-and-slide into that walk, so she tries to drop her gaze. Closer, so that he begins to smell the uncertain flower-garden mulch of her eau de toilette, her Christmas-gift scent, her bargain-bucket odour, and she can smell that he's one of those nice men who keep themselves clean, he smells of washed cotton shirt and shined-up shoes, of vicious soap and butch cool creams, and even the four-millimetre suede of his hair has gloss. Fastidious is what you call a man like that. She's next to him, placing the coffee cup, how good a wife she'll be one day, and she parts her knees a little so that his palm can travel up between them slowly, like an iron pushing creases flat. She meets his eyes now, and smiles; she will wait as long as he wants her to, until he types in those last messages, finishes talking to America, and he can come home with her for a while. There are others, she knows, there are high female voices on his answer-machine all day long, there are knuckle-muffled sobs, grating whines of worry, brief witty invitations, hard angry-voiced questions. She'll give up the day she hears the nightingale-call of tenderness in his voice when he talks to one of these women, when she senses the rainbow-burst of sincerity in what he's saying. But she knows that's not likely to happen. She tells all her friends that she has a sixth sense about people, a sixth sense. And he's just not the type to go off and fall in love with anyone.

PR is a good business. He likes the impersonality of the exchanges, the coolly political warmth of the links he's making. He has no friends – nobody in the business has friends – he only has these links, contacts, acquaintances, he hooks up, there are people who owe him a favour, there is a deal in the making. In this business, nothing is done simply because you like someone. Someone he used to speak with from the Juliane days called him at home. It was a once-in-a-blue-moon occurrence, as he likes to say, an in-house thing, a who'll-fit-the-job brainstorm. And this person, yes, owed him a favour.

And it was convenient, the job was a useful step – PR for fine art paintings, yin and yang, he likes to say – he was a viable option; so now he can look out of the window at the rest of Covent Garden, in his discreet office above a restaurant/bar, and look at the tourists, the trend-setters, the students, the fun-seekers, the style-chasers, those who believe in a young artistic sub-community and come here to find it. His PR sensibility tells him that Covent Garden is a good concept.

The things in the Turnpike Lane house are packed. The new clothes with their dark sheen, their lustre of quality, are pressed and folded; bowls and plates are piled in leaning newspaper towers; only the oak desk from the front room is coming with him, the rest of the furniture is being left behind. There is a place up in Hampstead, smaller, but with stripped floors and an intriguing spiral staircase and a converted loft. There is a small back garden and a high wall heavy with climbing plants, and in the mornings the place is a mobile slide-show of light. And you can see it rising from the floorboards, reverberating off the walls, shading down from the ceiling: the place reeks of quality, of authenticity. It is the real thing.

He has got a taste for fucking. One-nighters are his speciality, risky situations are his forte, the knee-trembler is his favourite. His pleasure is the stolen type. Is it Mandy, Emma, Karen? Was that Julia, Polly, Sam? Is it Carla, Simone, Peta on the phone? Is it Tabitha, Tess, Trudy he's meant to fax? He forgets their names all the time, but the women he screws are used to that. The women he fucks are the ones everyone fucks: they're PRs.

Nobody sees his home, and nobody will see the new house. In the humid stranglehold of June nights he thinks of his sister, as he did in the unruffled satin of spring evenings, the iron-clench of winter. Every night he wants her more badly. She has sent him a note, just one half-sheet of thin paper, a few weeks ago, telling him that she is 'expecting', that she is happy, and each stroke of each individual letter has planted a separate tumour of sad anger inside him. There are no synonyms for some words, none that do justice to the blunt reality. He is neither melancholy nor maudlin nor whimsical, he is not filled with ire, or incensed or riled. Sad anger is it. He knows, now, that she was right: his rage and hers. They would indeed burn the street down.

He's not a late-night person. He'll drive with a woman to some deserted corner after work, after the last get-together, after he's clinched the last deal, and sit in a cosy bistro with its cosy booths, her ankle scraping up and down his calf, but midnight will see him crouching in the bare darkness of the house looking through old magazines, old papers. Nearly all will be thrown out; he's not someone who goes through life jangling with mementoes from the past, with remembrances and reminiscences squeezing themselves out at every opportunity; no clattering trail of souvenirs skitters behind his heels. And he has to have his beauty sleep; the world of PR is a tough place to live.

While north London lies in its iron hermit's bunk listening to the strange calls of youth exploring the alleyways in the tangerine glow of streetlamps outside, Kensington glows whitely, serenely, with the passive calm of a sleeping child. No baseball-capped drug-eyed nutter jerks and shimmies along the pavements here, there's no threat of black-skinned hoodlums leaping with their tiger-vigour out from unnoticed hiding-places, no Asians loitering by stacked columns of empty cardboard boxes and kebab-spit on corners, no Greek kids in no damp-walled snooker houses. The rapists here wear port-coloured smoking-jackets and silk pyjamas, and do it to their wives; the murderers' faces are masked with clippered beards and a flop of geometric hair; the robbers have their eyes on more than a snatched handbag, and do it by Vodaphone. Drug-addicts snort coke off Philippe Starck tables. Adulterers don't go to the Virgin's Arms or the Beacon to find action, they accost their maids by the conservatory and suavely smack silent their Cantonese protests.

The residential side of Kensington is primly lavish, tucked beneath its veil of black iron gates, its scrub of house-alarm wires and intercoms, its night-porters and camera security, the electronic chastity-belt of the neighbourhood. Outside one house is an ant-colony of black cars, a cockroach-swarm of understated class on wheels, a shoal of shiny dark hammer-heads with leather interiors, floating in the expensive dark of Kensington. Out of the cars come women, collectively beautiful in their variety of necklines: tailored and square, sweetly heart-shaped, a straight Hepburn line from shoulder to shoulder, a stretchy low oval, a demure collarbone scoop. No woman has ugly shoulders. The fabrics and colours repeat themselves: satin embossed with whorls of walnut brown; velvet in alternating swatches of wine and grape; linen steeped in paprika dye; devastating twilight-blue shantung silk. All the rage, these days. The labels are a chant of the most-desired, a nursery-rhyme of the aspirational.

Inside the house, kindly lent by a friend, an industry buddy, everything is melting in a buttery cloud of social ease. From where he twitches and mutters in a corner, sweat damping and double-stamping every inch of his flesh, guts squeezed out dry an hour ago in the force of a dozen spring-tight retches, Will can see the mass slope of a hundred bared necks, the shine of a hundred careful hairstyles. He's not the only abuser here, not by far: there's a narcotic glint in most eyes, an alcoholic languor in most limbs. He's not the only one with a locked jaw and a nervous tic, not the only one who goes to the bathroom too frequently because he's scared of pissing himself in public. The men are a community of sombre linen suits whose shades vary minutely, a medley of the elemental: sand, stone, cement, olive, beech, pine, almond.

No man is ever happy at his own party; people come up to him, become distinct in their disengagement from the blurry mass of legs and heads, and wish him luck. *Electra's Dream* is out, *Electra's Dream* exists, a tiny bug-eyed baby formed out of runny dreams and gobbets of cash, sliding about in the muddy fluid of his supposed control. The moment it is out there, out here, Will realizes how small it is. In the paranoid monochrome thriller that now always runs in his head – flashing sirens, gnashing Rottweilers straining leashes, black leather coats and sharply tilted fedoras – every house on every cloistered Kensington street is hosting a faux-discreet launch party. For the past two weeks, the airbrushed face of every hoardings princess has buffeted his eyes, the wacky typeface of every advert, the anthemic music of every trailer has twanged and stuck like a dart inside his memory. His brain is an anthology of current releases, a micro-historiography of cinematic life, a directory of his contemporaries, a Yellow Pages of potential threat. So he eyes up the press-guys, the media boys, the hacks and pundits and moguls of the printed word who're here, forked tongues flipping out to lick lemon-peel lips, effeminate hyena-giggles contending with church-organ guffaws. The press divide into two types: the reptilian – spare, scaly, sidling around, looking about, ready to deliver that vindictive scorpion-sting – and mammalian, bovine, broadly moral, contentedly champing and chomping, feasting benignly on the cud of current affairs. There are others, of course, the integrity-guarders, the intellectually virile, the liberal family men, the spiky quirky women writers, but they aren't here.

He is never alone, during the evening. Right now, he is sitting next to a friend from his writing days, with his healthy wide neck and capable hands, the I-no-longer-drink bloom on his face, that smell of children and wife and dishwasher, and they float out together on a two-man rowboat of memories. Before, it was a woman, someone he has definitely screwed, probably, once or twice, with her forgiving words and her wedding ring, whose brassy ugliness he fixated upon, and he joked and nodded obligingly for her. Now and then people with whom he has worked for the last year pass by and wave gently, momentarily connected, they are the only ones who understand him, and see what he sees when he catches his own reflection in one of the broad square mirrors: lines in his face like knife-marks in cream cheese; old-paint cracks in his lips; crud lining his eyes, which hate the sight of the outside so much that they've retracted into their own dim world, where vision is secondary to their own motion, their tiny uplifts and twirls and pops, their wild arcs and rigid up–down invisible barcode movement, the secret code of seeing.

He is still beautiful, the beauty that improves with age, he still has that angularity, that anorexic doll's-grace, but his veins are a slowly clogging network, a railtrack where everything is becoming more and more delayed. Signals aren't reaching, messages aren't being received; some manic chemical highwayman is blocking the route. Sometimes he wakes up in the morning and can't feel his own hands or feet; they lie like blocks of cement muffled in cotton-wool bandages. His extremities have become a pale blue/purple, the lilac-lavender-rose of underwear and pot pourri. His hair is an oil-slick of secreted gunk, it smells of sleepless nights, while his breath smells of Dettol rinse and unwashed dog. His dick doesn't work anymore, except to release a jetblast of tangy razorblade-painful urine every hour.

He looks in the mirror for a long time, because his eyes aren't being obedient. He looks, he sees, he notes, he doesn't comprehend. But what he sees also is the non-attendance of the girl, the non-materialization of Ian, he sees ten mantelpieces of ten friends on which the thick cream square of his invitation is getting dustier, curly at the edges, is yellowing in that pile of takeaway pizza menus, of ancient clipped-out money-off coupons, of leaflets advertising window-cleaning. He knows that the printed word, the little card, has a built-in obsolescence; left long enough, it'll crumble back to nothing.

And he also sees and can't confront the image of the Lodge with its red eye darkened, with the sign outside whistling to itself in the late Hertfordshire wind, casting its shadow like a sundial throughout the day. He can see and can't confront the endless sweep of time that's taken the solid curve of trees from a wilting line of saplings to that protective barricade –

the cupped fist of bark and juicy leaf – the time that'll shrug and sweep on again past Juliane's departure, the still-standing house, until the white parachute of country sky finally folds down.

There is no more poetry in Will's brain, when it comes to this. There are certain things in life which defy language, there are certain reactions which are cheapened by metaphor, by reference, by quotation, which pale in significance when compared to the incontrovertible fact of their existence.

What shocks him most, beyond the baldness of what has occurred, is the method. He tries to imagine: the early-morning resolution, the fresh-eyed decision, the selection of the tie, the length of rope, the torn and knotted bedsheet, the boy-scout cutting and folding, the securing, the calculation of weight and speed. The physics of suicide. And then the final act, the jaunty circus-flip over the banister, the vault that every teenage boy perfects, the stretch of pressurized vertebrae, the squeeze of links struggling to stay connected, the final subsidence, the submission, the agonized breakage. That puppet-dance on the end of the string, that quizzical puppyish tilt of the head, the final rigid-backed convulsions, that slow half-turn, suspended in the air of the hallway, where light pours in and spreads across the glass tables and shining floorboards, birdsong travels high and fluting from the garden and in from the shady porch slide the violin-tones of jasmine.